Margaret

Born in Gainsborough, Lincolnshire, Margaret Dickinson moved to the coast at the age of seven and so began her love for the sea and the Lincolnshire landscape.

Her ambition to be a writer began early and she had her first novel published at the age of twenty-seven. This was followed by twenty-seven further titles including *Plough the Furrow*, *Sow the Seed* and *Reap the Harvest*, which make up her Lincolnshire Fleethaven trilogy.

Many of her novels are set in the heart of her home county, but in *Tangled Threads* and *Twisted Strands* the stories include not only Lincolnshire but also the framework knitting and lace industries of Nottingham.

Her 2012 and 2013 novels, *Jenny's War* and *The Clippie Girls*, were both top twenty bestsellers and her 2014 novel, *Fairfield Hall*, went to number nine on the *Sunday Times* bestseller list.

Margaret Dickinson

PORTRAIT OF JONATHAN

First published in 1970 by Robert Hale

This edition published 2014 by Bello
an imprint of Pan Macmillan, a division of Macmillan Publishers Limited
Pan Macmillan, 20 New Wharf Road, London N1 9RR
Basingstoke and Oxford
Associated companies throughout the world

www.panmacmillan.co.uk/bello

ISBN 978-1-4472-9010-0 EPUB
ISBN 978-1-4472-9008-7 HB
ISBN 978-1-4472-9009-4 PB

Copyright © Margaret Dickinson, 1970

Visit **www.panmacmillan.com** to read more about all our books
and to buy them. You will also find features, author interviews and
news of any author events, and you can sign up for e-newsletters
so that you're always first to hear about our new releases.

Author's Note

My writing career falls into two 'eras'. I had my first novel published at the age of twenty-five, and between 1968 and 1984 I had a total of nine novels published by Robert Hale Ltd. These were a mixture of light, historical romance, an action-suspense and one thriller, originally published under a pseudonym. Because of family commitments I then had a seven-year gap, but began writing again in the early nineties. Then occurred that little piece of luck that we all need at some time in our lives: I found a wonderful agent, Darley Anderson, and on his advice began to write saga fiction; stories with a strong woman as the main character and with a vivid and realistic background as the setting. Darley found me a happy home with Pan Macmillan, for whom I have now written twenty-one novels since 1994. Older, and with a maturity those seven 'fallow' years brought me, I recognize that I am now writing with greater depth and daring.

But I am by no means ashamed of those early works: they have been my early learning curve – and I am still learning! Originally, the first nine novels were published in hardback and subsequently in Large Print, but have never previously been issued in paperback or, of course, in ebook. So, I am thrilled that Macmillan, under their Bello imprint, has decided to reissue all nine titles.

Portrait of Jonathan, my third novel, was published in 1970 during the same week in which my first daughter was born.

'Man's love is of man's life a thing apart, 'Tis woman's whole existence.'

Don Juan—Lord Byron.

Chapter One

'You cannot possibly contemplate such a thing.' Giles Eldon thumped the table with his clenched fist to emphasise his viewpoint. The cut glass tinkled, the silver rattled and the candles flickered.

There was an uneasy silence around the table following his outburst, and, as he realised he had spoken out of turn, embarrassment spread across his young face. He saw that his mother had raised her fine eyebrows—she could not let her son's discourtesy in criticising their hosts pass without rebuke—but he saw too that her eyes belied the purse of her lips.

Giles relaxed a little—his mother, at least, agreed with him though she could not voice her unanimity. Giles glanced at his father and at his eldest brother, Jonathan. His father's frown was easy to read for he was seated on the other side of the table though not directly opposite Giles. His brother's expression was somewhat more difficult to discern for the latter was seated next to him and his head was inclined towards their hostess. Lady Sarah Kelvin. But he could imagine that Jonathan's face wore a similar expression of censure as their father. Lord Melmoth, Giles thought irritably. He was always in trouble with one of them, he mused, though 'affectionate' trouble he called it. He knew it was only his impetuosity which led him into difficulties. As a family they were devoted to each other: he could see that now after having spent but a few hours in this house and having seen the contrast between their family life and that of their hosts, Viscount and Viscountess Kelvin.

Giles' restless eyes returned to the cause of his outburst. The daughter, Lavinia Kelvin, was seated opposite him, her eyes downcast on her plate, upon which the food was almost untouched. She could not be more than fifteen or sixteen, he supposed, perhaps not even that, though she showed signs of blossoming womanhood. Her dress, no more than a child's party dress with short, puffed sleeves, frills and a wide sash, was too small for her. The blue silk was faded and, he could imagine, mended here and there. Her black hair was drawn tightly back from her face into two plaits looped around her ears. Her face was pale and plain. Her only appealing feature was her large brown eyes, which, Giles had noticed when she had dared to look at him—only once during the whole evening, held such a world of misery that the young man's ready pity was instantly aroused.

'And why not, pray?' The shrill voice of Lady Kelvin at the end of the table penetrated Giles' wandering thoughts. He turned his eyes from the girl to the mother. Lady Kelvin was a thin, shrewish-looking woman with eyes like a viper and a mouth to match.

'My son forgets himself, Lady Kelvin,' Rupert, Earl of Melmoth remarked, his low, cultured tones easing the tension somewhat. Giles, a little surprised, noticed that his father's tones held no note of reprobation towards him, and had he not felt some sympathy with Giles' view, then undoubtedly his anger would have been apparent.

Did the Earl of Melmoth agree with his younger son then? And, Giles thought, what of his brother?

It was an ill-assorted gathering, Lord Melmoth mused, and one which came together for the first time, and probably, as the evening progressed unfavourably, for the last. Their host, Lord Kelvin, who lounged at the head of the table, was the only son of Wilford Kelvin, Earl of Rowan, a close friend and business partner of Lord Melmoth, who together formed the 'Keldon Shipping Line'. The chief occupation of their fleet was tea-transporting from China. On receiving the invitation to dine with 'young Kelvin's family', the Earl of Melmoth and his wife had been thrown into somewhat of a dilemma.

'But my dear,' Evelina had spread her expressive hands, 'what can they want of us?'

'Hmph,' the Earl had grunted, ' "want of us" is a good way of summing up this little invitation, my love. Undoubtedly, Gervase Kelvin is short of money, as always, but 'tis the first time he has presumed upon my friendship with his father and approached me.'

'Are you going to accept the invitation, Rupert?'

'I wish I knew how things stood between Rowan and his disreputable son—there would be my answer. If they are reconciled now, my refusal would hurt Rowan, and that I would not have for the world. And yet, if the gulf is as wide between them as ever and the quarrel still on, then my acceptance is almost insulting to my friend.' He had sighed. 'A predicament, my love, to be sure.' He had tapped his pursed lips with his forefinger.

'I think,' he said slowly after a moment's pause, 'it would be diverting to accept and see what the young man has in mind.'

The 'young man', however, whom the Earl had not seen for some fifteen years, had changed beyond recognition. It was almost impossible for Lord Melmoth to believe that this man was his friend's son, so dissimilar were they.

Gervase, Viscount Kelvin, was obese in his figure, gluttonous in his manner and totally lacking the finesse which his birth demanded. He was a disgrace to the family name of Kelvin and, in particular to his long-suffering father. He had caused Lord Rowan a great deal of unhappiness, anger and final disillusionment, Melmoth knew. He remembered the frequent occasions—years before—when Rowan had confided in him on his fears regarding his son.

'He is totally lacking in every characteristic which I admire in a man, Melmoth. I can never allow him to join the "Keldon Line", that would only add to my worries,' Lord Rowan had said dispiritedly. 'But what *am* I to do?'

This particular conversation which Melmoth remembered now, had been caused by Gervase's unsuitable marriage to Sarah, a girl who, though of good parentage, was far too weak-willed to be of assistance to her dissolute husband.

'This will kill his mother,' Lord Rowan had said in anguish and sure enough, within six months of Gervase's marriage, his mother, a sweet and charming creature, was dead.

That, Lord Melmoth thought, was the beginning of the final break between father and son. Instead of trying to mend his ways, Gervase had gambled more, drank heavily and had relied more and more upon his father to pay his debts and support his family. Within eight years of their marriage, five children had been born to Gervase and Sarah, Melmoth recalled, but only the first two had survived, the three younger children dying before they had scarcely drawn breath. As a young man Gervase Kelvin had possessed a moderate degree of good looks and charm, and with the advantage of his birthright, he should have embarked upon a distinguished career. But his character was sadly lacking in the qualities so necessary to achieve distinction. How two persons of the calibre of Lord Rowan and his beautiful wife could have produced such a son was a mystery to all who knew the family intimately—and it was a life-long source of mortification to Lord Rowan. Gervase Kelvin had slipped from careless youth into rapacious manhood. His choice of marriage partner was a disaster, but there was little Rowan could do to prevent the union. Sarah had never been even pretty: her thin face with its sharp features, beak-like nose, darting eyes and narrow lips, and five children within eight years had left her thinner and more haggard than ever, her tongue sharper, her voice whining and petulant.

Lord Melmoth's eyes turned towards the children of the marriage. The eldest, Lavinia, was a pathetic creature and shown no affection by her parents—all their love (if they were capable of such a worthy emotion) was showered upon their son, Roderick. He was a pale, pimply youth with a weak chin and deceitful eyes. During the hour or so he had been under their roof, Melmoth had summed up the situation. The girl was ill-used by the other three—so much so that on entering he had thought her the maid for she had opened the door to them and had helped to serve dinner, and it was not until she had taken her place at the table that he, and he was sure the rest of his own family too, had realised with a shock that she was the daughter of the house.

The Earl could not help but compare this family with his own. As he glanced, with affection, at his wife she looked up and caught his eye. He knew, with that inexplicable rapport between man and wife, that through her mind were passing the very same thoughts which possessed him. Evelina, Lady Melmoth, was a picture of serenity and elegance and on her beautiful face all the kindness and generosity which was her nature was shown. Melmoth revelled in his good fortune at having met such a woman and never ceased to marvel at their happiness, and he guarded the affection of his family jealously.

Melmoth's eyes moved to his eldest son, Jonathan, Viscount Eldon. He was now twenty-seven, and, Melmoth thought, it was high time he was married. Jonathan had been rather wild in his youth, of course, Melmoth reminded himself, but only natural, high spirits, nothing—degrading, like Gervase Kelvin. Of course Jonathan had become entangled with that flighty girl, Anthea, who had treated him so cruelly and had finally married Lord Thorwald, a man over twice her age but extremely wealthy. Had Jonathan really loved the girl or had it been merely youthful infatuation? Melmoth sincerely hoped it had been the latter for the girl was not worth Jonathan's affection. Melmoth smiled ruefully. The boy could never forget her, though, whilst he bore that scar down his left cheek which, rumour had it—though Jonathan had never divulged his secret to a soul as to how he had come by it—that he had fought a duel over the girl. Duel indeed, Melmoth almost snorted as he remembered his anger at the time. But that had been the last of Jonathan's wild escapades for since that time he had passed straightway into manhood and he was indeed a son to be proud of now: sometimes perhaps a little *too* serious, such a change from one extreme to the other. Perhaps he still cared for Lady Anthea—Melmoth sincerely hoped not.

His attention turned to his younger son, Giles. He was beginning to participate in the same wild escapades in which Jonathan and he himself in his youth, Melmoth had to admit, had indulged in. Still, there was no harm in the boy and age would rectify these faults—he was merely impulsive and impetuous.

There was a marked contrast between the appearances of the two brothers. Jonathan was tall and thin with brown, wavy hair and dark brown eyes. His face, once boyishly handsome, had thinned a little too much so that his cheeks were hollowed and the ugly scar down his left cheek marred his looks. His mouth, usually serious, could flicker into a smile somewhat lopsided now because of the scar, thus giving him an almost cynical twist to his smile. But his eyes were warm and kind. Over his dress he was fastidious and the cut of his clothes was immaculate—a little dark and sombre, Melmoth mused, for he himself had lived in an age of more dandified styles for men, and the latest trend In men's dress where trousers, tailed coat and even waistcoats were all of the same sober, dark hue, did not appeal to Lord Melmoth. But, he had to admit, his son Jonathan wore such clothes with a quiet air of distinction. Giles, on the other hand, wore his clothes—a little more colourful and flamboyant—with a careless, and yet somewhat dashing, air. He was not as tall as Jonathan though by no means short, broad like his father, with fair, curly hair and side whiskers. He was ever seen to be laughing, his blue eyes twinkling merrily, and Melmoth sometimes despaired of Giles ever accepting the responsibilities which life would undoubtedly hold for him. He was for ever in a scrape of some kind needing the calming influence of either Lord Melmoth or Viscount Eldon.

Tonight's outburst was a typical example of Giles' impetuosity. But, Melmoth admitted, this particular incident could not arouse the anger of either himself or Jonathan, for undoubtedly they both found themselves in agreement with Giles.

A remark by Lady Kelvin had provoked Giles' violent disagreement.

'Lavinia is to dine with Lord Myron tomorrow evening, Lady Melmoth. I have great hopes of an alliance between Lord Myron and my daughter, though I must admit she is sadly lacking in the kind of qualities and beauty Lord Myron admires.' She paused, glancing disdainfully at her daughter. 'But for some reason he *seems* to find her attractive.'

Her voice held a note of incredulity, and the girl blushed in embarrassment at having her person discussed with guests.

'You are all dining with Lord Myron tomorrow night?' Lady Melmoth said conversationally.

'Oh no. Lord Myron specifically asked that Lavinia should dine with him alone.'

There was an uneasy pause before Giles broke the silence angrily.

'You cannot possibly contemplate such a thing!'

Chapter Two

When the ladies had withdrawn leaving the gentlemen to their port, Lord Melmoth tried tactfully to broach the subject with Lord Kelvin.

'Do you think it wise, Kelvin, to allow your daughter to visit Myron completely unchaperoned? He is—ahem—er—not quite the sort of man to know how to treat a young girl.' Melmoth almost smiled at his own understatement of the case.

Lord Myron was a lecherous old devil, in whose company no woman, and least of all a young, naive girl, was safe. Besides which, Myron was a business rival of Melmoth and Rowan, running a tea-transporting line of clipper ships in partnership with Lord Thorwald. Lady Anthea, in spurning Jonathan's affection in favour of Lord Thorwald, had dealt him the double blow in allying herself with the rival company. Competition between the ships of the two lines was fierce and Melmoth was not convinced that their rivals were above underhand dealings. In fact, at the first mention of a proposed liaison between Lavinia Kelvin and Lord Myron, Lord Melmoth had immediately wondered what mischief lay behind the scheme.

Gervase Kelvin was up to no good, and would, Melmoth feared, cause even more heartbreak to his father. However, he thought as he sipped his port—cheap port it was too—no doubt he would find out soon enough for it was now obvious that he and his family had been invited to dine with some definite purpose in view.

Melmoth glanced round the room. Only the area around the table was well-lit leaving the surrounding parts of the room in shadow. To a purpose, he thought, for he could discern that the furnishings were shabby and no doubt the silver upon the table was the last vestige of the wealth to which Gervase Kelvin had once had access. Now, his source of income stopped, the family had moved from house to house each time having to lower their standards until they had come to this—a furnished house in a middle-class part of London, with time-worn furnishings and personal clothing. No doubt Kelvin was after lining his coffers by compromising his daughter with Lord Myron. Heaven help the poor child! thought Lord Melmoth at once finding himself in total sympathy with his youngest son's earlier outburst.

'See no reason why not,' Kelvin was saying, breathing heavily, his florid face redder than ever, though whether from excess of food and drink or embarrassment, Lord Melmoth was unsure.

'But I didn't ask you here to talk about that,' he continued.

'No?' Lord Melmoth murmured. Here it came, the reason for the invitation.

'Truth is, Lord Melmoth.' Kelvin spoke almost respectfully for once, Lord Melmoth noticed, smiling inwardly. He tapped his lips with his forefinger and waited for his host to continue.

Kelvin's face grew hotter. 'Truth is, I'm in a bit of a strait, y'know. I was wondering—what I mean is—you know how things are between my father and me. I was wondering if you'd have a word with him.'

Melmoth remained silent.

'Fact is, I'd like to come into the business, y'know. After all, I'm his only son,' he added righteously. 'Your boys will inherit your share, surely I'm entitled to something?'

True, thought Melmoth to himself, a resounding good hiding if I am any judge. Still he remained silent, whilst Gervase Kelvin grew more and more flustered.

'Well,' he asked, almost defensively, 'will you?'

'Will I—what?' Lord Melmoth asked mildly.

'Speak to my father?'

The Earl of Melmoth appeared to meditate whilst Viscount Kelvin grew even more agitated. Melmoth saw that his two sons watched the proceedings with absorption—Jonathan with his slight sideways smile, and Giles, his blue eyes, puzzled, darting from face to face anxiously, not understanding the full depth of meaning behind the scene. Roderick Kelvin's face remained as vacant as ever.

'Yes,' Lord Melmoth said slowly, 'I will speak to your father.'

'Soon?'

'I cannot say for sure—we are not due to meet for a week or more.'

'Can't you make it sooner than that—I'm depending upon you?'

But at that Viscount Kelvin would have to be satisfied for Lord Melmoth refused to be harried into giving a certain date for seeing Lord Rowan. Had Kelvin any idea, Melmoth thought to himself, of what he meant to tell Lord Rowan, then he would doubtless have been begging him to forget the whole idea. As it was, Gervase Kelvin seemed heartily pleased with his efforts and when they rejoined the ladies he was in great spirits, even calling his wife 'my dear' which appeared to startle and displease her. The only object of her affections appeared to be her pimply son.

'Come and sit here, Roddy, beside me and Lady Melmoth and tell Lady Melmoth how you absolutely adore riding. He's *such* a good horseman. Lady Melmoth. It was such a pity we had to sell our horses. However, I am hopeful things may yet take a turn for the better in the future,' and she glanced at Lord Melmoth as if to insinuate that the family's well-being lay in his hands.

'And your daughter,' Lady Melmoth was saying. 'Does she ride?'

'Lavinia—good heavens no! She is a sad disappointment to us. Lady Melmoth, though I am loath to say it of my own child. She is completely without accomplishment.'

And as every eye turned to look at her, poor Lavinia blushed scarlet and could have rushed from the room in shame.

Poor child, mused Melmoth, such an innocent scrap to be sacrificed to Lord Myron's lechery. He began to study her unobserved. Although at first glance she appeared plain and uninteresting—insipid he would have said—on closer inspection, Lord Melmoth saw that she had a flawless complexion. Her hair, so unbecomingly dressed, was as black and glossy as a raven. Her sorrowful brown eyes were fringed with long, curling lashes. But she was so thin—under-nourished almost—that she looked only a child. Lord Melmoth found himself worrying about the girl's visit to Lord Myron planned for the next evening.

Could he do anything to prevent it?

He turned his gaze away from the girl and as he did so, his glance met Jonathan's eyes which at that very moment had also turned from Lavinia.

Instinctively, Lord Melmoth knew that the very same thoughts possessed his son as himself.

The Eldon family took their leave of the Kelvin household as soon as was politely possible. Immediately they were within the confines of their carriage and a safe distance was between them and their hosts, Giles once more burst forth.

'Sir, can you do *nothing* for that poor girl?'

Lord Melmoth sighed before he replied. 'My boy, I too have been racking my brains to think of some unobtrusive way in which we could prevent her dining with Myron, but short of resorting to tactics which would obviously be interfering, I can think of nothing, can you, my dear?'

Lady Melmoth's gentle tones replied. 'It seems we are all of one mind, that is if Jonathan feels as we three do?' She paused and waited for her son's answer.

'Of course I agree with you,' came Jonathan's soft voice out of the darkness. 'But I too cannot suggest a solution.'

'The girl is no more than a child,' Lady Melmoth said, adding with disgust, 'it is positively wicked!'

'She's like her paternal grandmother, poor Mélanie,' murmured Lord Melmoth.

'Rupert, no,' his wife countered. 'Mélanie was a great beauty—this poor child is plain.'

'No, dear Mama, the child has promise,' Jonathan's deep, slow tones remarked.

'You saw it too, then?' said his father. 'With a little help and affection that child would be quite delightful. But she's utterly starved of attention and affection, anyone can see that. All their love, if you can call it that, is showered upon that—that apology of manhood.'

'But what are we going to do?' repeated Giles.

But the other three occupants of the carriage had no answer for him.

The next evening by the time they anticipated that Lavinia would be on her way to visit Lord Myron, they still had no solution.

The whole family was disturbed. Giles paced the long drawing-room restlessly. Jonathan tapped the arm of his chair with the tips of his fingers, and Lord Melmoth pretended to read, but so infrequently did he turn a page that to the intelligent observer it would have been apparent that he found concentration impossible.

Only Lady Melmoth, seated on the brocade chaise-longue—a pole-screen shading the heat of the fire from her face, seemed calm and unruffled. Serenely, she stitched at her embroidery, the silks flashing in and out of the material held firmly by a wooden frame. But a moment's lapse of concentration caused her to prick her finger and admit that she too was not intent upon her occupation.

'There must be *something* we could do. She—she might be there by now,' Giles said. His father laid down his book, cleared his throat and pulled the gold watch from his waistcoat pocket.

'Most likely she'll just be arriving.'

'They'll sit down to dinner almost immediately, I would think,' Jonathan murmured.

'Then what?' Giles murmured. His mother bent her head over her embroidery. Giles turned towards his father, who cleared his throat again and picked up his book, Giles turned at last to Jonathan who met his gaze steadily.

Jonathan rose.

'I think. Father, there would be no harm if Giles and I were to take a drive past Lord Myron's house?'

'No, no, my boy, of course not—it's a free highway.'

'And Lord Myron's house is conveniently situated near the road,' Lady Melmoth murmured, her needle stabbing in and out of her work rapidly.

'Come, let's be off,' cried the impatient Giles, flinging the door wide and rushing into the hall, followed more sedately by his brother, the half-smile twitching at his mouth despite the gravity of his thoughts.

They took their own brougham and the younger of the family's two drivers as the most likely to match the brothers' desire for speed.

The dark streets echoed with the horses' hurrying hooves. The January night was clear but cold and frosty.

'Why do you suppose Lord Myron dines so late?' Giles murmured.

'We dine early by some standards. But I rather think, in his case, he dines late because it suits his particular purpose.'

The two brothers fell silent, both, no doubt, imagining just what that 'particular purpose' was.

After about half an hour's drive, Giles leaned forward to look out of the window.

'This is the street. Is it this side, Jonathan?'

'Yes,' and he too leaned forward to look out.

The driver slowed the horse to walking pace, as Jonathan had previously instructed him. Most of the houses had lighted windows. It was not a part of the city the Eldons knew well, but the district seemed to be of equal standing to their own. Lord Myron's house was easy to pick out being the largest and bearing on its wrought iron gates the name in bold lettering 'Myron Court'.

'There it is,' said Giles in a loud whisper.

The windows of the house were alight but the curtains were drawn across and nothing of the interior of the rooms, nor of their occupants, was visible to the onlooker.

Jonathan cursed under his breath. Short of somehow gaining entry to the house, they were no better off here riding up and down a darkened street than they would have been at home, and just as helpless.

Their vehicle turned at the end of the street and went back the way it had come, the occupants changing to the opposite window.

'We'd better go home, Giles,' Jonathan said. 'We can do no more here.'

'Just once more down the street and back,' pleaded Giles.

'All right.'

It was on the second return up the street that they saw her, a small figure in a white dress running, without cloak or bonnet, through the heavy gates of 'Myron Court' into the street.

'Stop, Wilkes,' roared Jonathan and with one accord they jumped from the brougham, one out of each side, and ran towards Lavinia. Jonathan reached her first, having chosen the nearer door.

The girl stopped as she saw him and gave a frightened shriek. In the light of the street lamp, he saw immediately her tear-streaked face, her dress torn at the shoulder and her black hair disarranged and flying loose.

He felt a rash of pity for the child and at the same time as wanting to comfort her, his anger against Lord Myron was sufficient to have called him out to fight a duel there and then. But the girl was his foremost thought. He stretched out his arms towards her. She screamed again and stepped backwards. Giles came running up and Lavinia's terror increased. She sobbed hysterically backing away from them all the time.

'Lavinia,' Jonathan said sharply. 'Lavinia, control yourself—it's Eldon—you remember, we dined with you last night.'

The sobs subsided a little but she still hiccoughed pathetically, straining her eyes in the darkness to see who they were.

'We mean you no harm,' Giles was saying gently. 'We only want to help you.'

She stood still then and allowed them to approach her, and stand one on either side. She looked up into their faces in the light of the street lamp. Then she covered her face with her hands and wept, but without hysteria now, merely in relief and thankfulness. Jonathan placed his coat about her shivering shoulders and led her towards the brougham.

As they sped towards 'Eldon House' Lavinia burled her face on Jonathan's shoulder and wept bitterly, whilst he, his arms about her, stroked her hair tenderly.

And that was the moment when Lavinia fell in love with Jonathan, Viscount Eldon.

Chapter Three

When they arrived at 'Eldon House', it was Giles who gave a graphic account of their rescue of Lavinia to Lord and Lady Melmoth, whilst the subject of his conversation clung to Jonathan's arm, not daring to meet their eyes.

'My poor, dear child,' Lady Melmoth's voice lacked nothing in kindness and sympathy. 'Rupert, my dear,' this in a low tone to her husband, 'I think you should call Doctor Benning.'

'Do you think it wise, my dear, I mean—the scandal if . . .?'

'I do think it *most* necessary,' Lady Melmoth said firmly.

Her husband, ever respectful of his wife's intelligence in such matters, agreed.

'Now,' she said briskly to the weeping girl, but not unkindly. 'Come with me, my dear, and well put you to bed. You've had an unfortunate experience, but you must put it out of your mind now and try to forget it. Come.'

Talking kindly to the girl. Lady Melmoth led her away, whilst the three men watched their departure from the room.

'Well, well, I'm sure I don't know what the world's coming to,' muttered Lord Melmoth as the door closed.

Jonathan shrugged and poured himself a glass of wine.

'Unfortunately, there's always been Myron's type about, prepared to take advantage of youthful innocence.'

'He ought to be run through,' Giles exclaimed glowering savagely and thrusting his right fist into his left palm as if he were giving himself the pleasure of duelling with Lord Myron.

Jonathan fingered the scar on his cheek.

' 'Twould serve no purpose,' he remarked mildly, forgetting

momentarily his own similar feeling when first seeing the distraught figure of Lavinia running from Myron's house.

'Jonathan, how can you be so calm about it—that—that seducer and that poor girl? I should like to see him at the end of a sword for sure.'

'Question is,' Lord Melmoth mused, 'what to do with the child now?'

'I'm sure Mama has that all in hand, Father,' Jonathan smiled his half-smile.

'Ha, yes,' his father chuckled fondly, 'no doubt, no doubt.'

Some little time later, Lady Melmoth rejoined them in the drawing-room.

'She's sleeping now. The doctor has been.' She closed the door and walked across the room, whilst three pairs of eyes followed her movement. 'And he says she is badly shocked, but quite unharmed.'

The three men grunted their approval, so alike in their manner.

'What are we going to do now?' asked the ever-impatient Giles of his mother, who, in her turn, looked towards her husband.

Lord Melmoth's blue eyes twinkled at her merrily.

'Well, my dear, and what *are* we going to do?' he asked, knowing full well she had already decided.

'Well,' smiled Lady Melmoth, guessing her husband's thoughts as exactly as if he had spoken them—thus had their marriage brought them to such a degree of understanding. 'I have been thinking that we should keep her here—for a day or two at least. We can send some message or other to her parents.' Lady Melmoth dismissed them as of no consequence. 'And then, I think, we should contact Lord Rowan about her.'

'What?' Lord Melmoth looked up sharply. 'Do you think we should? After all, the girl will scarcely know him since her father and grandfather have been estranged for so long. And,' he cleared his throat in some embarrassment, 'Rowan may not want to be troubled about her.'

'If we but get him to see her, that will be enough,' she replied and noticed Jonathan's quiet smile.

'Why?' asked Giles. 'Why just if he sees her?'

'My dear boy,' his mother replied, 'you wouldn't realise, but Lavinia is so like Lord Rowan's wife, Mélanie, he could not refuse to care for her—he could not find it in his heart to do so. I did not see the likeness before, Rupert, but I do now.'

'Oh,' said Giles.

'Mmm,' mused the Earl, whilst Jonathan merely smiled to himself.

So it was that the next day Lord Melmoth, taking his elder son with him for support, found himself undertaking a journey of over a hundred miles to Lord Rowan's country residence in Warwickshire. They made the journey leisurely, being in no great hurry, and stayed overnight en route to arrive at 'Avonridge' the following afternoon.

Although the Earl of Rowan and Lord Melmoth were business associates, Lord Rowan as the older and more senior partner took a less active part in the day to day running of their trade and now that Lord Melmoth's sons had both joined the business, the Earl of Rowan was content to allow the affairs to rest comfortably in the capable hands of the three Eldons. Of course, he was kept fully informed of all important transactions and consulted on all major matters—but his 'working' days were far behind him, and instead he lived alone, save for his servants, in his country mansion, heartily weary of the pressures and disappointments of city life.

'Be just the thing for Rowan, y'know,' Lord Melmoth said suddenly after many miles of silence.

'Mmm?'

'To have Lavinia live with him. Just the thing—far too lonely the fellow is, all alone in that great palace of a place in the middle of the countryside. *Just* the thing.'

'Mama is right, then?' Jonathan smiled.

'Your mother's always right—well,' Lord Melmoth chuckled, 'chose me, didn't she?'

'How are you going to tell him about Myron?'

'Lord knows,' the Earl groaned. 'What a thing to have to tell the chap.'

And their journey continued in silence.

Had their minds not been so preoccupied with the unpleasant task ahead of them, the journey would have afforded them much pleasure for in the pale, wintry sunlight the countryside through which they passed was a delight. Serene, undulating hills and fields with slow winding rivers and patches of woodland, and the villages of thatched cottages and tudor houses—all gave the impression of gentle beauty and peaceful harmony.

'Avonridge' lay in its own parkland through which the river Avon ran. Deer raised their heads inquisitively as the carriage wound through the grounds to the house itself set on the highest point of the land belonging to the Earl of Rowan.

Lord Rowan was surprised, but delighted to see his friend and colleague, for though the Eldon family were frequent guests at 'Avonridge' it was unusual for the Earl to arrive without invitation.

'This is an unexpected pleasure, Melmoth,' Lord Rowan said as they were shown into his study. The Earl of Rowan was a tall, distinguished-looking man, with an almost military bearing. His voice was deep. His silver hair was still abundant for a man of his years, springing from his broad forehead, above bright blue eyes which could change with surprising swiftness from sternness to twinkling mirth, or vice versa. His manner was ever-charming though somewhat reserved, and his one trait was to twirl the fine points of his moustache.

Melmoth and Rowan were very similar in character and manner, though Melmoth lacked Rowan's inches in height and consequently his more dignified bearing. Melmoth too was somewhat careless in his speech whereas Rowan's cultured words were always precisely pronounced. He was the epitome of dignity but wholly devoid of any air of pomposity. That his sternness was often more apparent than Melmoth's was, perhaps, caused by the various blows which life had dealt him, firstly in the disappointment in his only son and then the grief at his wife's death. Now, loneliness was his greatest enemy, for whilst he shrank from the rigours of city life, it was apparent that there was still something lacking in his secluded country life.

But now Lord Melmoth thought he had found the answer.

'Tell you the truth, Rowan, it's an enforced visit,' Melmoth began before he had even sat down. He was inclined to be impatient like his younger son and could not bear to delay when something was worrying him.

'Trouble?' Lord Rowan's eyes were sharp.

'Well—yes, you might call it that.'

'What is it, one particular ship or the whole fleet?'

'What? Oh no—nothing to do with business, my dear fellow, nothing at all.'

The Earl of Melmoth settled himself comfortably in an armchair whilst Jonathan went to stand before the long windows which looked out over a smooth lawn sloping down to the banks of a stream which wound its way to join the Avon.

'Really?' Rowan's eyebrows lifted slightly, but he waited for his friend to continue. He merely signed to his butler to bring his guests refreshment and settled himself in the armchair opposite Lord Melmoth and waited.

'It's family trouble. Rowan.'

'Ah!' Lord Rowan sighed. 'I'm sorry to hear that, Melmoth,' he glanced briefly at Jonathan's stationary figure at the window and added quickly, 'but you know I'll do anything I can to help.'

'What? Oh Lord no! I mean,' said the flustered Melmoth, 'not *my* family, dear fellow, yours.'

There was a moment's pause before Lord Rowan sighed again, leant back in his chair, his elbows resting on the arms, his fingertips touching.

'Tell me the worst, Rupert,' he said resignedly, using his friend's christian name which he did rarely and only in moments of intimate friendship.

'I'm not putting this very well, but it's rather difficult, so bear with me, please.'

Lord Melmoth recounted the full story to Lord Rowan starting with the invitation from his son, Gervase Kelvin, and ending with

Lavinia's visit to Lord Myron, and the reason for their journey to see him. At the point in the tale when Melmoth touched, though lightly in order to try and save his friend's feelings, on Lavinia's visit to Lord Myron's house, he saw Lord Rowan stiffen in his chair and in his eyes was an expression of rage and disgust.

'She's not harmed though, Wilford, we made certain of that,' the Earl of Melmoth hastened to reassure him.

'That makes my son's part in it no less shameful,' Lord Rowan muttered.

'You cannot blame the girl—she is far too young to realise what was happening,' Melmoth added.

'No,' Lord Rowan sighed, 'no, poor child, she is but an innocent victim. And you say Gervase had the audacity to ask to join our Company?'

Melmoth nodded. 'I don't understand it, Wilford, if he's trying at the same time to ingratiate himself with our rival, Myron.'

'He's about some underhand practice, I don't doubt,' Rowan replied, and Melmoth was prompted to feel sorry for the man who must, of necessity, speak ill of his own son in such a way. The bonds of family affection are hard to break, but in the circumstances of all the past and now this latest incident, Melmoth could not be surprised that Rowan had little feeling for his son.

'Forgive me, Lord Rowan,' Jonathan had moved from the window, 'if I presume too much, but do you think it possible that your son could be trying to be taken into our Company for—er—spying purposes?'

'Quite likely, my boy. But what prompts you to think this?'

'I heard—two or three years ago it is now—that your son was *already* an associate of Myron and Thorwald, so why, unless he's been thrown out—which is unlikely as Lavinia was being sent to Myron—should he interest himself in our concern?'

The two older men exchanged a look.

'I think you have a point, Eldon. But surely, if that is the case, he would not have wanted you to know about Lavinia's proposed visit to Myron.'

'True, but he may be relying on the fact that he thinks we do not know of his association with their Company. I recall that at the time I heard about it, it was only a vague rumour and, quite honestly, would have remained so had I not made it my business to find out—discreetly—whether there was any truth in it,' he smiled.

'And was there?'

'Oh yes. Of course, he held a very junior position and, from what I could gather, they treat him rather shamefully as regards payment of salary.'

Lord Rowan laughed but without humour. 'I doubt my son's services are worth very much, Eldon. No doubt they only allowed him to join them in the hopes that his relationship to me could prove useful to them. I'm glad you told us, my boy.'

'I did not do so before, sir,' Jonathan replied quietly, 'for I did not wish to cause you greater disappointment—and I would not have done so now but for the unexpected turn of events.'

'But what of Lavinia?' Lord Melmoth prompted.

'I suppose legally I cannot force her away from her parents—but I rather think that if she has failed in her mission to Myron—and thank God she has,' he added fervently, 'then my son and his wife will have little further use of her. I shall count on that being so.'

'Will you have her here, then?' Melmoth asked.

There was a slight pause before Lord Rowan replied.

'I suppose I have little choice—she is my grand-daughter, but having recollections of her parentage, I doubt we shall have much in common,' he sighed wearily, anticipating further trouble and heartache ahead of him, this time caused by his grand-daughter.

Lord Melmoth and his son exchanged a glance and by mutual silent consent decided not to enlighten Lord Rowan as to Lavinia's true disposition. It would be better for him to find out for himself.

Whilst her husband and son were making their journey, Lady Evelina Melmoth was absorbed in her self-appointed task of caring for Lavinia. She had taken the girl to heart immediately and was determined to bring some pleasure and comfort to the child's life. In this she was ably assisted by the kind-hearted Giles.

Lady Melmoth allowed Lavinia to sleep late the morning after the night of her unfortunate adventure and so Lord Melmoth and Viscount Eldon had departed without seeing her again.

'Now, Giles,' said his mother when they had breakfasted. 'I would like you to help me. I propose sending a message to the Kelvins explaining that their daughter is a guest in our house and that we shall be pleased to have her stay with us for an *indefinite* time.'

'Shall you tell them anything about last night?'

Lady Melmoth gave an uncharacteristic snort of disapproval.

'I most certainly shall *not*. I propose to ignore the whole affair. Let them find out how she came to be here for themselves.'

Giles sighed. 'Lord Myron will no doubt have acquainted them with the truth by now. Perhaps they're worried by her disappearance.'

'I very much doubt that. However, I am not concerned with those wretched people only with their most unfortunate daughter. I shall take her a breakfast tray myself very soon. Then, when I can, I shall find her some pretty dresses—I might even call my dressmaker in. The poor child is so thin I doubt whether any of my gowns would fit her.'

'Do you know how old she is?'

'Ah, now let me see, she was born about the time her grandmother, Lady Rowan, died. That would be about eighteen years ago. Yes, she'll be seventeen or eighteen.'

'Really—she only looks about fourteen.'

'The child has obviously been slow to mature because she has been given no encouragement or advice. To think what she must have suffered!'

Mother and son lapsed into silence.

'Do you think she would go for a drive with me?' Giles murmured.

'I shouldn't rush her, Giles. Let us not forget what a terrifying experience she had last night. She may not want to see *any* man for some considerable time.'

However, when Lady Melmoth awoke her protégé with a prettily-laid breakfast tray, she found the girl much improved. Lavinia was certainly quiet and most painfully shy which was evidenced by the slight stutter in her speech from time to time, but all trace of the hysteria and fear she had suffered the previous evening was gone. She merely seemed overcome with gratitude towards her rescuers and to the kind Lady Melmoth. The only cloud on Lavinia's immediate horizon appeared to be her impending return home, but when Lady Melmoth imparted her proposed plan to her, the girl actually smiled and the brown eyes lost their haunted look—though only for a fleeting moment.

Lady Melmoth found she enjoyed the entire day. She sent for her dressmaker who promised several dresses for Lavinia as soon as was humanly possible and, once Lavinia's protests were brushed aside. Lady Melmoth and the dressmaker took complete charge and Lavinia was not consulted at all as to style or material. Indeed, there would have been little point, for the child, though well-spoken and well-mannered, was sadly lacking in knowledge of such matters. Lady Melmoth supposed.

When Lady Melmoth found herself alone with Giles for a few moments she told him, 'Giles, I have had a reply from the Kelvins—they are *delighted* to have their daughter stay with us for a time and thank us most kindly for our hospitality.'

'Thought they would,' Giles grinned.

Lady Evelina wrinkled her smooth brow.

'The only thing which worries me is that it may provoke them to think we want to strike up a closer liaison with the family, which, of course, we do not.'

Giles groaned.

'However,' his mother continued briskly, 'we'll leave *that* side of it to your father and Jonathan. We must concern ourselves with Lavinia herself.'

Lord Melmoth and Viscount Eldon were not expected to return for four days, but perhaps it was as well. Lady Melmoth thought, for Lavinia was so nervous and solemn. Even the ebullient Giles could only manage to raise a smile from her once or twice—a thing unknown amongst the fair sex when in his company.

Lady Melmoth said little but watched the two young people with an indulgent eye. Giles and Lord Rowan's grand-daughter, she mused, now I wonder? Here her brow creased as she was reminded of the fact that should Lord Rowan—though she could scarcely contemplate such a thing—refuse to take his grand-daughter into his care the Melmoths would be thrown into a proper dilemma. But never one to dwell upon gloomy thoughts. Lady Melmoth contented herself that her husband and elder son would not fail in their mission—they could not.

The next day brought bewilderment and unexpected pleasure for Lavinia. The dresses arrived for her—the dressmaker must have been stitching through the night to have completed them in such a short time. There was a morning dress of green and white stripes, crinoline in style but not so voluminous as those worn by Lady Melmoth herself. She could see that Lavinia had no idea of present fashion nor knew how to handle tie wide, sweeping skirts, having been kept in child's dress by her mother. The blue afternoon dress was trimmed with white lace on the sleeves and a lace collar, and the evening dress which Lavinia would be expected to wear at dinner was pale pink silk with short puffed sleeves, the crinoline skirts being decorated with bows of darker pink ribbon.

'For me, for me,' Lavinia whispered, her brown eyes searching Lady Melmoth's face, incredulously, as each parcel revealed such treasures as the girl had scarcely seen before and certainly never possessed.

'Of course, my dear. Come, try them on. Oh, how I *love* new dresses, don't you?'

'I—I've never had any—not Hike these,' Lavinia murmured, though in complete honesty and with no trace of sympathy-seeking in her voice.

It was surprising what a difference the new gowns made to her appearance.

'Now, when I've dressed your hair in a fashionable style, my dear, you'll be quite a young lady.'

Lady Melmoth arranged Lavinia's hair parted in the centre with a coil at the back, but leaving three or four ringlets over each ear—a softer, prettier style than that she normally wore.

Lavinia stared at herself in the long mirror—her fingers moving nervously over the dress material.

'I've never worn anything so—big. I—I don't know how to walk in it.'

'Just take a turn about the room—slowly, child, slowly, head high—don't look down at your feet or you will stumble. That's it, small steps and your skirts follow you, see?'

'Yes, yes. Oh, it's so b-beautiful.' She turned and came towards Lady Melmoth who saw tears glistening in the girl's eyes. 'How can I ever thank you?'

'Nonsense, child. To see you pleased with them is thanks enough.'

'Pleased! I am overwhelmed.'

When they went downstairs to join Giles in the drawing-room, he, with the frankness of youth, was quite unable to conceal his astonishment at the change his mother had wrought in Lavinia's appearance within a few hours. She was quite passably pretty now—transformed from childish styles to blossoming young womanhood. But to Giles, already stricken by a feeling of protectiveness for the innocent, maltreated child, she now appeared with added charms on the threshold of womanhood.

'How pretty you look, doesn't she, Mama?' he said taking Lavinia's hand in his and placing it through his arm. 'Why Jonathan and Papa will scarcely recognise you.'

At this the girl blushed, but Giles was not to know that it was not his compliment which brought the colour to her face, but the mention of Jonathan's name linked—however slightly—with her own.

Lady Melmoth and Giles found it necessary to keep up the flow of idle chatter for Lavinia seemed shy to the point of awkwardness.

'I shall take you for a drive tomorrow if it's not too cold and show you the sights of London—but I am forgetting, you live here. Perhaps you have seen all there is to see.'

The girl smiled wistfully. 'I scarcely think so, sir.'

'Don't call me "sir", for goodness sakes. Reserve that for my father—or old Jonathan—if you must, but at least call me Giles.'

The following three days passed in much the same manner: Lady Melmoth assisting Lavinia with her appearance and Giles exerting all his charm to entertain their guest and take her mind off her unfortunate experience. The drive through the city proved successful—Lavinia appeared to enjoy it, though Giles did most of the talking. Once or twice he managed to make her smile and so he considered his time well-spent. He found himself constantly thinking of ways in which he might bring a smile to her face and a light to those sad, brown eyes.

Late afternoon of the fourth day brought the return of Lord Melmoth and Jonathan.

'Ah, my dear,' said the Earl entering the drawing-room, his hands outstretched to his wife, who was alone in the room, Giles and Lavinia being out driving once more.

'Ah, Rupert, you are returned safe and well, I trust?'

'Yes, yes, my dear.'

'And your trip was successful?'

'Well—er—now. I must tell you all about it, but first allow me to change from my travelling clothes—the roads are long and dusty.'

'Of course. Jonathan, my dear,' Lady Melmoth said as Viscount Eldon also entered the room. He kissed his mother affectionately on the cheek, and stood back to look at her, his strange smile playing at the corner of his mouth.

'Mama has been enjoying herself, eh sir?'

'Eh what—mmm?' Lord Melmoth turned back from the doorway. 'Why shouldn't she enjoy herself, eh?'

But mother and son exchanged a secret smile whilst Lord Melmoth disappeared up the wide stairs muttering to himself.

'But,' Jonathan was saying softly, 'we know just *how* she has been enjoying herself, don't we, dearest Mama? And how is your little fledgling?'

'Jonathan, my dear,' Lady Melmoth put her hand on her tall son's arm, 'you'd never believe the change in the girl—she is quite a young woman once divested of those childish clothes and adorned in something more befitting her age.'

'And just how old is she?'

'I haven't asked her, but she must be seventeen or eighteen. Giles is quite captivated by her,' Lady Melmoth laughed.

'Is he indeed?' Jonathan said rather shortly and turned away abruptly. 'I too must change before dinner,' and he left the room whilst his mother's puzzled eyes followed him.

What, she mused, was going on in the mind of her taciturn son?

For a few moments before dinner the Eldon family found themselves together before Lavinia appeared.

'Now, Rupert, tell me of your visit to Lord Rowan.'

'Well, m'dear, Rowan was distressed at what we had to tell him—as I had imagined he would be. . .'

'But did he say he would help the child?'

'Well—yes,' Lord Melmoth said slowly. 'You don't sound too sure. Surely he did not refuse—she is his grand-daughter?'

'He was not *un*willing, my dear Evelina, but somewhat doubtful of the success of such a move. Remember, my dear. Rowan hardly knows his grand-daughter. He has not seen her for a number of years and therefore has no notion of the girl's adult character. He can only—unfortunately—compare her with her parents and in so doing is apprehensive. No doubt he fears she will bring similar trouble to him as her father before her did.'

'Ah, I understand,' his good wife said gently. 'But did you not tell him of the resemblance between Lavinia and her grandmother, Mélanie?'

'No, my love. I thought of it—but decided that it was best that Rowan should find the likeness himself—it will be a pleasant surprise for him after all his pessimistic thoughts. And besides, there were other reasons. For one, I thought he would not believe me, perhaps think that I was trying to sway his decision by playing on his love for his wife—and for another, *we* do not know the child's character well enough. She appears harmless, but . . .'

'Papa, Lavinia wouldn't hurt a fly, she's a sweet girl and has been cruelly used,' Giles burst out, his young face hot with indignation.

His father turned his twinkling eyes on Giles.

'My, my, Lavinia has found herself a champion and no mistake. Calm down, my boy, I meant no insult to the child. I was merely trying to explain why I found our visit to Lord Rowan difficult.'

'I'm sorry, Papa, but she's so—so lost and helpless. She does so need someone to take care of her.'

The other three members of the family looked at Giles, no doubt all wondering whether his interest in the girl was becoming more than just the desire to help her.

'Well,' said Jonathan, 'she'll soon have Lord Rowan. Despite his reluctance, he has said he will take her to live with him.'

'But he wants to leave it for a week or two,' continued Lord Melmoth. 'He would like her to stay here for the moment and then he will come up to London, meet her and take her back with him.'

'And what about her parents?' Lady Melmoth reminded him.

'Ah, now they might present the greatest difficulty, of course. But Lord Rowan has said he will see Gervase. An unenviable task—it won't be easy for him.'

'I wonder what bargain Gervase Kelvin will try to hold his father to,' Jonathan said softly.

'Bargain, what do you mean, bargain?' asked the Earl.

'I still think Gervase is up to something. Their invitation the other evening to dinner was proof. I cannot imagine he will let the matter rest there. Even if he allows her to go now, I think that at some time in the future he will try to use her—especially if Lord Rowan becomes fond of her, as we expect he will.'

At that moment the door opened timidly and Lavinia appeared.

' 'Pon my soul,' the Earl said, 'is this the same child, Evelina?'

'Yes, Rupert,' his wife replied, with pride in her voice. 'Come, my dear,' she continued turning towards Lavinia, 'and sit by me.'

The girl moved forward smiling tremulously at Giles, who grinned broadly at her. She glanced quickly, with frightened eyes, at Jonathan, whose half-closed eyes followed her progress across the room, and then she lowered her gaze swiftly.

'We've been to see your grandfather, my child,' Lord Melmoth said kindly as Lavinia seated herself beside Lady Melmoth and arranged her skirt carefully.

'M-my *grandfather?*' The wide brown eyes regarded him with surprise. 'Lord Rowan, you m-mean?'

'Yes, and he's coming up to town next week to meet you.'

'Oh no—I mean—he cannot possibly mean to meet me. We—I mean—my father is . . .' she plucked nervously at the material of her dress, 'estranged from Lord Rowan.' The girl hung her head as if the shame of the family quarrel were all her own.

'We know all about that, my dear,' Lady Melmoth said kindly, taking Lavinia's cold hand in hers and patting it comfortingly. 'You do not have to explain to us. Do you know that Lord Melmoth and your grandfather are business partners?'

She nodded. 'Yes I have heard Papa speak of it.'

'Have you indeed—and what did he say?' Lord Melmoth's tone held a note of sharpness, unusual in the mild-tempered man.

'He was t-talking about three weeks ago, about inviting you to d-dine and said—and said . . .' She paused a moment as if unable to continue, whilst the four members of the Eldon family waited attentively.

'. . . he said he wanted to c-cultivate your friendship to try and get you to take him into the Company, but,' and she raised her brown eyes and regarded Lord Melmoth steadily, 'I really cannot understand why because he is already engaged in business with Lord Thorwald and Lord Myron.'

'Ah,' said the Earl, with a wealth of expression in his tone, 'we thought as much!' He slapped his thigh triumphantly.

Lavinia looked from Lord Melmoth to Lady Melmoth, to Jonanthan and lastly to Giles, fear written in her face.

'Have I said s-something I should not have done?'

'No—no,' Giles said quickly hurrying to her side. 'Anything you tell any of us here goes no further. You may trust us, you know, Lavinia. Can't she?' he demanded of his family.

Her smile was a little uncertain still. Jonathan strolled languidly to the centre of the room from his usual position in a chair by the window.

'Of course she can,' he said in his slow, deep tones, but never glancing once in her direction. But when Giles turned back to Lavinia he found her gazing at Jonathan like a rabbit mesmerised by a stoat, and he too followed her gaze and regarded the straight, solemn figure of his brother.

Chapter Four

During the following two weeks, before Lord Rowan made his proposed visit to London in order to make the acquaintances of his grand-daughter, two events took place which had some effect on Lavinia's life.

The first, and perhaps the one which was to have the greatest effect on the young girl and cause her a deal of unhappiness, happened three days after Lord Melmoth and Jonathan returned home.

Lord Thorwald, the senior partner in the Company which was the rival to the Keldon Line, and his wife, Lady Anthea, were invited to dine at 'Eldon House': an unusual occurrence but for a reason.

'We'll play them at their own game, my lord,' said the roguish Earl of Melmoth to his wife in the privacy of their bedroom. 'If we can't bring the whole business into the open, we must resort to their tactics to try to find out what is going on.'

'But what of Jonathan having to meet Lady Anthea again?' asked his wife with worried eyes.

'Ah—hum, yes, well, he need not be present if he wishes otherwise. Silly business, all that, wasn't it, my dear?'

'Yes, Rupert—it could have been disastrous—and even now I am not sure just how Jonathan feels about it all. Don't forget he bears the scars to this day, and always will, of his—affair—with Anthea.'

'Now, Evelina, you know as well as I do, no one *knows* for certain how Jonathan came by that scar—it may be a lot of romantic nonsense that he got it fighting a duel over the woman.'

'If it was not a duel, my dear Rupert, why was Viscount Selwyn out of society for two months, supposedly laid low with fever, if he was not recovering from a wound inflicted by Jonathan?'

'Was it he Jonathan was supposed to have fought? I had forgotten.'

'Viscount Selwyn was besotted with Anthea and because Anthea seemed to favour Jonathan the more, Selwyn called him out.'

'And Jonathan came off best and so he won,' Lord Melmoth said proudly.

'That makes it no less foolhardy,' Lady Melmoth said firmly.

'Evelina, it is all a long time ago, all of eight years, is it not? Viscount Selwyn recovered.'

'Yes, but he never married and neither has Jonathan. Anthea married Lord Thorwald—for his money I don't doubt.'

'Then she's the bigger fool of the three,' snorted the Earl.

'But why has Jonathan not married?' said Lady Melmoth slowly. 'Is it because he can find no woman to match Anthea in his heart?'

'Nonsense,' replied her husband. 'It's just that he has seen more sense—hasn't found the right woman. That business sobered him up, you must admit that, he was a bit of a young rip before.'

'Yes, yes, he was—though you wouldn't think it to see him now. And poor Giles would be too if he had not got both father and elder brother to quell his high spirits.'

'Truth is, my love,' said Lord Melmoth kissing his wife's forehead. 'Jonathan cannot find a woman to compare with his mother.'

'Rupert, really.' But she was pleased by his flattery.

Lady Melmoth continued to worry about her elder son. It was high time he was well-married and producing a son and heir. She sighed, fastened a pearl necklace about her throat and regarded her appearance in the mirror with satisfaction yet without conceit.

At the same moment, Lavinia too was seated before the mirror in her room. Tears welled in her eyes as she looked at herself. What a plain creature she was. She could not even wear this beautiful evening gown Lady Melmoth had bought for her to any advantage, she thought. Her hair had been expertly dressed again by Lady Melmoth's personal maid, but Lavinia was so unused to a fashionable style that she held her head rigidly for fear the pins would loosen should she move her head quickly and her hair come cascading down to her shoulders. The dinner party before her would be an ordeal. Lavinia did not mind so much now dining with just the Eldon family, though she was still in awe of Lord Melmoth and as for Jonathan, she hardly dare to glance in his direction for fear he should see her adoration for him plainly written in her eyes.

Tonight, she thought, she would have to face these guests and, to make matters worse, Lord Myron and her father were connected with them in business. She felt as if she were being caught up in some kind of intrigue which she could not understand and her only salvation she felt, lay with the Eldon family whom she trusted instinctively.

But what would happen, she thought unhappily, when she was obliged to return to her parents to be bullied as before, used by them as a pawn to ingratiate themselves with such repulsive people as Lord Myron? Lavinia sighed heavily, dried her tears and walked stiffly towards the door, bracing her shoulders for the evening ahead of her.

The guests had not arrived by the time that the family and Lavinia had gathered together in the drawing-room. Lord and Lady Melmoth made such a handsome couple, Lavinia thought enviously. He was so distinguished-looking and she so beautiful and elegant. What a contrast to her own parents. If only these two charming, generous persons were her parents, she mused longingly. But then, if they were, Jonathan and Giles would be her brothers, and whilst she could welcome the latter in such a role, the last relationship she would wish for with Jonathan was as a brother. She knew she could never hope to win him as a husband, but nevertheless even a plain girl can dream, she thought.

Jonathan was as immaculately dressed as ever. The black tail coat and trousers, contrasted with the white waistcoat, shirt and bow tie, seemed to make him taller and more severe. Whilst Giles wore much the same style of clothes, though his shirt was frilled whereas Jonathan's was plain, he wore his with a more casual air and lacked the elegance of his brother.

'Vinny, you look positively charming,' Giles grinned, took her hand and kissed it in mock gallantry.

Lavinia, somewhat startled by his approach and at the unusual shortening of her name, smiled nervously and blushed, but Giles' display had given her a little confidence and she did not fear the evening quite so much as she had done previously. She even dared to meet Jonathan's steady gaze instead of dropping her eyes in acute shyness.

'My Lord and Lady Thorwald,' announced the butler in sonorous tones and the Eldon family turned to greet their guests. Lavinia too turned towards the door, interested to see these people whom she knew to be involved with her own father and Lord Myron in business. At the thought of the latter personage, she shuddered involuntarily. To her surprise, Jonathan must have noticed for he moved to her side and smiled down at her quickly before turning back to greet the guests.

As Lady Anthea made her entrance, Lavinia gasped. She had never seen such a ravishingly beautiful woman. Of course, Lady Anthea was dressed in a gown of emerald green silk trimmed with white lace and styled in the very latest fashion. The neckline was low and the bodice tight-fitting but, Lavinia noticed, the skirt was not quite the usual crinoline shape being flatter in front but voluminous at the sides and forming a train. Lady Anthea's hair—a rich auburn colour—was dressed in an elaborate style high on her head but with curls framing her face. She was undoubtedly the most beautiful woman Lavinia had ever set eyes on, but, she thought, Lady Anthea's green eyes were rather hard and her mouth held a hint of cruelty.

Lavinia could not help but notice, as no doubt did everyone else in the room, that Lady Anthea's eyes immediately sought Jonathan, whilst he returned her gaze steadily, a small, amused smile at the corner of his mouth.

Overwhelmed by Lady Anthea's beauty as Lavinia was, the sight of Lord Thorwald caused her the greater surprise. He was all of seventy—in fact he appeared even older. He was a small man, much smaller than his wife—a fact which was emphasised by his stooping frame. He was painfully thin, his hands claw-like, the blue veins sharply etched upon the back of his hand.

'My *dear* Lady Melmoth,' Lady Anthea was saying in deep-throated tones. 'How *nice* to see you again. So *kind* of you to invite us to dine and so unexpectedly too. Oswald dislikes entertaining, you know, so my social life has been sadly neglected.' She moved on, with similar inane words to Lord Melmoth and thence to Jonathan, as if, Lavinia thought shrewdly, she had not meant to seek out Jonathan particularly from the moment she stepped into the house.

'Jonathan, my dear,' she purred, stretching out her hands to him, which he took in his, but after a moment's hesitation.

'How are you, Anthea?' A slightly cynical note in his voice was apparent.

She grimaced. 'Bored my dear, but well in health. And you—how are you?'

'Far from bored and quite well, I thank you.'

Anthea pouted, her eyes flirting outrageously with him. Jonathan turned and introduced Lavinia to Lady Anthea.

'This is Miss Kelvin,' he said.

'How do you do, my dear.' Lady Anthea's hand was limp in Lavinia's, and her eyes flickered briefly and disinterestedly over Lavinia. 'Are you being allowed to stay up late to dine with us—what an honour for us?' Lady Anthea laughed cruelly. The remark heard by everyone in the room did not appear to amuse anyone else but Lady Anthea, and Lavinia herself blushed scarlet and hung her head.

Giles was by her side in a moment. 'Come over here, Vinny, and sit with me.'

Taking her arm he led her to the far end of the room but over his shoulder he exchanged an angry glance with his elder brother. Jonathan, the smile gone from his face, wore an expressionless mask, but deep in his eyes was a strange look as his gaze followed the figure of the young girl, whose head was bowed, her shoulders hunched as if she had been dealt a hurtful physical blow.

'Come, Jonathan,' Lady Anthea's soft voice tried to lure his attention back to her, 'we have much to catch up on, have we not?'

Giles led Lavinia over to the piano out of earshot of the rest of the conversation.

'No doubt we shall have to suffer Lady Anthea's playing after dinner,' he said.

'If she plays as well as she is beautiful,' Lavinia said wistfully, 'it should not be a sufferance.'

'Don't envy her, Vinny. She's not worth it, especially after what she had just said to you.'

She looked up at Giles' face, which was unusually serious.

'You sound bitter, Giles—surely not on my account.'

He sighed. 'Partly—and partly not. It's an old story. Jonathan was in love with her several years ago and we thought she loved him, but she treated him shamefully. There was a quarrel over her between Jonathan and Viscount Selwyn. Rumour had it that that was how Jonathan got his scar, but he has never admitted it. However, that seemed to finish it—Jonathan would have no more to do with her and soon after, she married Lord Thorwald—obviously for his money and title.'

'And Jonathan,' Lavinia asked in a small voice, 'what of him?'

Giles shrugged. 'I don't know. He doesn't show his feelings at all now—if he's got any. But seeing him now with her again, I wonder ...'

Lavinia followed his eyes to where Jonathan and Lady Anthea stood, oblivious of the others in the room, it seemed. Lady Anthea was talking softly looking up into his eyes, whilst Jonathan listened with that curious smile playing at the corner of his mouth once more.

In that moment, Lavinia felt her heart breaking over Jonathan.

The second event which had a profound effect upon the young girl was directly concerned with Jonathan.

During the week following the dinner party, Lavinia saw very little of Lord Melmoth, Jonathan, or, for that matter, Giles. Usually the whole family were only gathered together at dinner and for a short while afterwards. Her days were spent with Lady Melmoth, or alone in her room, where, unbeknown to the Eldon family, she pursued her favourite pastime of sketching, which she had always done in secret. Her parents, having once seen her sketches, had jeered at her efforts—unjustifiably so too, for her talent in that direction was considerable for a girl of her years, especially in view of the fact that her work was always done in secret and without encouragement or advice.

One evening after dinner, when the gentlemen rejoined the ladies in the drawing-room, Jonathan seated himself beside Lavinia, setting the girl's heart thumping painfully. She kept her eyes firmly fixed upon her hands in her lap, her fingers twisting nervously.

'Would you like to see our clipper ships at the docks, Vinny?' Jonathan asked, so softly that she could hardly hear him, and his use of the pet-name which Giles had bestowed upon her startled her even more than his unexpected suggestion.

'Oh, y-yes, I sh-should, please.' She raised her brown eyes to meet his.

'That's settled then. Tomorrow afternoon I have some time to spare and we shall go. Not a word to anyone, mind.' He smiled his curious smile, his voice little more than a whisper. 'I want you to myself for once.'

Abruptly, he rose and left her. Her eyes followed him, worshippingly, as he crossed the room to talk with his father. Would tomorrow ever come? She was fearful that the promise of an afternoon in his company would surely never come to pass.

But the following afternoon found her seated beside Jonathan in the brougham, her cheeks pink with excitement. She was wrapped warmly in a fur-trimmed cape which Lady Melmoth had given her.

The East India Docks, which she had never visited before, were a different world to her. The wharves seemed cluttered with cargo being unloaded from the tea clippers. Cranes lifted the tea-chests and boxes from the shops on to the wharf, and then the men with running-barrows methodically moved the chests again, though how, she wondered, they knew where everything was or where it should go, she could not imagine. Voices filled the air—instructions from those in charge, with replies, sometimes, of disagreement if the order was impracticable. Horses harnessed to carts stood patiently whilst receiving a load. The men were dressed in work-a-day clothes, many in shirt sleeves and cloth caps, some had a leather apron over their trousers. Here and there smartly dressed gentlemen in top hats and frock coats stood watching the proceedings. They must be shipowners, Lavinia thought.

'Take my arm lest you slip, Vinny—mind that rope.'

Shyly she put her arm in his and although the surroundings captivated her attention, she was nevertheless conscious the whole time of his nearness. The masts of the sailing ships lined up along the wharves resembled a forest of tall, straight trees. Jonathan pointed out the ships belonging to the Keldon Line.

'Do they only carry tea, Jonathan? Surely it is a wasted journey if they go from here empty?'

He smiled down at her. 'No, they take a great deal of merchandise from this country on their outward journey—almost everything you could think of: lead, iron, cottons. And of course, on the return although the main cargo is tea, they also bring other merchandise back—silks and so on.'

They walked on. The sight of the clippers enthralled Lavinia, not only because they were Jonathan's ships, but the thought of them travelling gamely across the wild oceans captivated her romantic imagination.

'Come,' said Jonathan. 'I want to show you my pride and joy.'

Eagerly she followed him as they returned to the brougham to travel a short distance.

'This is Blackwall,' Jonathan explained as the vehicle drew to a halt once more, 'where ships are built.'

They walked some distance amongst the workmen—carpenters, blacksmiths and joiners. Jonathan greeted many of them by name and they grinned and touched their caps to him. It seemed he was a regular visitor here and was popular with the shipbuilders.

'Here we are.'

Above them rose the enormous skeleton of a ship in the process of being built.

'We're keeping to much the same graceful shape of the clipper ships, Vinny.'

As Jonathan spoke, Lavinia looked up at him. His eyes were afire with enthusiasm, and his gaze roamed over the lines of the unfinished ship caressingly almost. It was obvious to her, in a moment, that all his hopes and dreams were bound up with this ship.

'But she will be fitted with a compound steam engine, which we hope will mean she should be able to travel from China to England non-stop.'

As Lavinia seemed puzzled Jonathan continued. 'You see the steamships are having a hard fight to prove themselves against the clippers. They have to carry huge quantities of coal—which naturally takes up valuable cargo space, or they have to make frequent stops to refuel, and that can cause a lot of difficulties in various ways. But with this more economical engine plus the fact that the Suez Canal will be opening soon—the steamship will begin to prove itself.'

'I see, and will the clipper ship be useless then?'

'Oh no—they'll last for many years and be worthy craft, but gradually they will be superseded by steam, there's no doubt about it. But all changes of this nature don't happen overnight. It takes years of gradual development, of trial and error by the inventors and a good deal of risk on the part of the shipping companies like ourselves.'

'What are you g-going to call her?' Lavinia asked.

'We haven't decided yet—it will be some time before she is launched, they've only just well begun. But I had wondered about "Mélanie" after your grandmother.'

'My grandfather is involved with the s-steamship then?'

Jonathan nodded.

'He must be a very—forward-thinking p-person,' she murmured.

'He is. He's a wonderful man, Lavinia. You'll like him.'

Lavinia looked away, none too sure. She was afraid of the proposed meeting between herself and her grandfather, and, even more, she feared her return home to her parents, which must be inevitable once she had met her grandfather. But with determined resolve she put such dismal thoughts from her mind and continued to enjoy her precious afternoon spent with Jonathan.

On their drive back home, Jonathan pointed out various places of interest to Lavinia.

'But I am forgetting, Vinny, you live here, you must have seen these places a hundred times and here I am showing them to you as if you were a stranger to London.'

'No—I haven't seen them before—truly. Mama does not believe in visiting p-places of interest. I've heard about them, of course, and occasionally seen such places as the Tower or the Houses of Parliament and even Buckingham Palace. But it's not the same as really visiting them for that purpose. I try to read as much as I c-can, but it's not always easy. Papa says it is a waste of time educating a girl and Mama says all the m-money for an education must go for Roderick.'

'Poor child,' Jonathan murmured under his breath and hoped that above the rattling wheels of the brougham Lavinia had not heard him. He could not bring himself to answer her. He was so overcome with anger against her thoughtless, selfish parents that he could think of no suitable reply.

Lavinia fell silent too. But the glow of the afternoon remained with her for a long time and indeed helped her to face the meeting with her grandfather with a little more equanimity.

The day arrived all too soon for Lavinia for she wished her stay with the Eldons could last for ever, and the meeting with her grandfather, she imagined, would terminate her stay here. She felt sure she would then be despatched home to her parents, and that the Eldons had, in fact, only extended their hospitality to her until her grandfather had met her.

In her room, dressed in the blue afternoon dress Lady Melmoth had bought her, Lavinia heard the carriage arrive. She could not bring herself even to peek out of the window—so afraid was she that he was a terrifying person. A few moments elapsed. Then she heard the maid's footsteps outside the door and her soft knock.

'Will you come down now, please, Miss Kelvin? Lord Rowan has arrived.'

'Y-yes.'

The footsteps moved away. Lavinia remained sitting before her mirror as if rooted to the dressing-table stool. She could not move, fear held her captive. But she knew she must go down. She could not disgrace the Eldons who had been so indescribably kind. They wanted her to meet Lord Rowan so she would do so.

The length of the stairs seemed all too short whereas normally it seemed interminably long. Lavinia paused outside the door of the drawing-room and took a deep breath. She reached for the knob with trembling fingers.

'Oh!' she gave a startled cry. Someone had come up from behind her and taken her hand.

She looked round to meet Jonathan's brown eyes and see his small smile.

'Don't be frightened, Vinny. He can't help but love you.'

Before she could reply, he opened the door and led her into the room.

Chapter Five

Lady Melmoth was seated on the sofa looking up at her husband and a stranger who stood together in front of the fire. Giles stood behind his mother. He turned and smiled at Lavinia as she entered with Jonathan. But immediately, Lavinia's eyes went to the stranger. He was an elderly man, but so tall and straight that his appearance belled his age. His hair was silver and he had a moustache which ended in two sharp points.

Lord Rowan turned, mid-sentence, and caught sight of Lavinia's small figure standing beside Jonathan, almost shrinking towards him for protection.

Her huge brown eyes were riveted upon her grandfather's face. Instantly, he saw the likeness between this child and his wife, Mélanie. Although this girl was only a shadow of Mélanie's beauty and personality, he could see at a glance she was a potential beauty. What chance had she had, he thought angrily, with Gervase as a parent?

Lord Rowan had stopped speaking without finishing his sentence, losing concentration as his attention was caught and held by the sight of his granddaughter.

'Here she is, sir,' Jonathan was saying leading her forward.

She came, unwillingly. Lord Rowan could see, to stand before him and submit to his scrutiny. She had lowered her eyes now and was looking at the floor, afraid to meet his gaze.

He cupped her chin with his strong fingers.

'Don't be afraid, my dear,' he said softly.

She raised her eyes slowly to look into his blue, clear and honest eyes, which were at one and the same time stern but kind. He

41

smiled down at her and Lavinia felt the warmth of his regard. She smiled back tremulously and in that moment there was created a bond of affection and mutual trust, nothing would or could ever break.

All in that moment, Lavinia knew she had found someone she could depend upon, someone who would care for her and care about her. Lord Rowan too realised that here was a child so unlike her parentage that it was as if they did not exist but that she was his own daughter—his and Mélanie's child.

'Sit down here beside me, my dear, and tell me about yourself—we have many years to catch up on, have we not?'

'Yes,' she said shyly.

'Well,' Lord Rowan said, though not unkindly, 'I'm waiting.'

'There's n-not much to tell. I haven't any of the usual accomplishments—all the money was spent on a tutor for Roderick. Papa considers it unnecessary for a girl to be educated—though I can read and write legibly,' she added, anxious not to disgrace herself immediately in his eyes. 'And l-love sketching, though I do it in secret. Papa and Mama do not approve and Roderick laughs at my efforts. You—you w-won't tell them, will you?' Her brown eyes were pleading.

'No—no—I won't tell them.' There was a strange catch in Lord Rowan's voice. Even though Lavinia had said all this without a trace of self-pity for she had merely stated the situation as it was, she little realised how pitiful it sounded to her listeners.

'I know a lot of places in London. Giles took me driving—and the docks and the clippers and even the new steamship—Jonathan t-took me.'

'Well, now, it seems that your education during the past week or so in the hands of these two fine young men has improved,' Lord Rowan teased, and Lavinia blushed. 'But I am going to suggest taking you away from them.'

The look of misery which came to Lavinia's face could not help but wring the hearts of all in the room.

'You mean—I m-must go home?' she whispered.

'Home with me, I mean, back to Warwickshire.'

'To "Avonridge",' her face brightened a little, 'for a holiday?'

'No,' Lord Rowan touched her hair gently. 'No, not for a holiday—for good. I want you to make your home with me, if you would like to do that.'

'Like it—like . . .' But she could not go on for tears of happiness choked her.

'There, there,' he soothed, putting his arms about her. 'Are you so averse to the idea?'

'Oh no, no,' she cried fiercely, throwing her thin arms about his neck and holding on to him so tightly as if she would never let go. 'It's the most wonderful thing that could ever happen.'

Her words ended in an emotional squeak, so overcome was she by her good fortune, and everyone in the room laughed, though kindly thus relieving much of the drama of the moment. Lavinia, through her tears, laughed too and burled her head against her grandfather's shoulder, smiling happily to herself.

So it was settled between them, her parents being considered a secondary problem. In fact, Lord Rowan paid a swift and unexpected visit to his son's dwelling, putting forward the proposition and extracting agreement from the spluttering Gervase and the nervous Sarah, and leaving before they had time to retract their consent.

Lavinia seemed perfectly happy to make the break with her parents and brother without even seeing them again and this, to Lord Rowan and the four members of the Eldon family, whilst pitiful, served to emphasise the misery she must have suffered under her parents' roof. No doubt the last act of their misuse of her—using her as a pawn in a tactical game with Lord Myron—had severed any bonds between Lavinia and her parents.

A few days later, Lavinia left 'Eldon House' with Lord Rowan to journey to her new home in Warwickshire, her only belongings being the clothes given to her by Lady Melmoth and a few sketches. Although Lavinia already loved Lord Rowan dearly, she could not help but regret leaving 'Eldon House'—the kindly Lord and Lady Melmoth, the gay Giles and, of course, Jonathan, whom least of all she wished to leave. She was heartened by the fact that Lady

Melmoth pressed her to come and stay with them again any time she felt so inclined, and also to hear Lord Rowan giving open invitation to the Eldons to visit 'Avonridge'.

The journey was long but of infinite interest to the girl and Lord Rowan was amused by her obvious delight in the countryside and all the sights and sounds which were so unfamiliar to a city-dweller.

They made the journey leisurely enjoying frequent stops and an overnight stay at about the half-way stage.

'Oh, the trees and fields!' Lavinia was ecstatic in her praise, and lost much of her shyness in her enthusiasm. The days were cold, but bright, and the countryside was peaceful and welcoming to the child from the smoke and dirt of the city.

At last the carriage turned off the road through wrought-iron gates which were opened by a man who rushed out from a small cottage near the main gates. He touched his cap respectfully to the occupants of the carriage. Lavinia saw two small girls staring at them from the cottage windows—it was a tiny cottage, whitewashed, the windows painted black with a thatched roof. On up the lane through magnificent parkland. Deer raised their heads questioningly.

'Oh Grandfather—is all this yours?'

'Yes, my dear. Do you think you can be happy here?'

'It's wonderful—wonderful.'

'There's the house—see through the trees.'

As they neared the house itself, Lavinia saw that it was rather severe-looking but nevertheless charming. It was square from the front, but the centre section was set back a little, the front entrance being exactly in the centre. Swiftly she counted the windows—there seemed to be so many—twenty, and then there were eight tiny dormer windows jutting out of the roof.

Round the main door ivy grew softening the harsh lines of the building. The drive curved in a semi-circle before the house, but the smooth lawns were divided by paths and trees. Neatly trimmed hedges bordered the driveway.

The interior of the house, Lavinia found, as Lord Rowan led her inside, was even more luxurious than the Eldons' town house. She felt a little overwhelmed by the ornate, painted ceilings, the panelled doors and wide, sweeping staircase. She was unaccustomed to grandeur of this standard.

Lavinia gazed around her and at last she glanced up at Lord Rowan to find him watching her.

'Welcome home, my child,' he said softly, and she read the tender affection in his eyes. 'This house has been lacking something ever since your grandmother died. Now, with you here, I can see what it was. It will be a home once more from now on.'

Lavinia blushed at the compliment. She was unused to such demonstrations of affection—indeed she was unused to being loved and she found it strangely moving to be welcomed into these beautiful surroundings and to realise that at last she belonged somewhere and to someone.

If only Jonathan were here, her happiness would be complete. Be thankful, she reminded herself sharply, for your present good fortune.

'Here's Mrs Matthews, my housekeeper, to welcome us,' Lord Rowan was saying.

A buxom, middle-aged woman appeared in the hall. The smile on her rosy face was wide and cheerful. She wore a plain black dress, with a white lace collar, but her welcome belied the severity of her dress. She bobbed a curtsy.

'Good afternoon, your Lordship, you're a little earlier than we expected. Did you have a pleasant journey, sir?'

'Yes, thank you, Mrs Matthews. This is my grand-daughter about whom I told you, Mrs Matthews. Have you prepared a room for her as I requested?'

'Yes, sir. Everything's ready.'

'Go with Mrs Matthews, Lavinia.'

As Lavinia stepped forward towards the stairs, she heard her grandfather say in undertones to his housekeeper, 'Treat her kindly, Mrs Matthews. She has had an unfortunate time.'

'Yes, sir, of course. Poor lamb!' The woman clucked sympathetically. She turned and came after Lavinia who was ascending the staircase uncertainly.

'Now, you come with me, my dear. I expect you're quite worn

out with all that travelling. You've got a lovely room at the front of the house, not far from his Lordship's room, overlooking the park.'

The woman chattered on in kindly tones, until Lavinia could not help but feel welcome.

As she reached the last curve of the staircase which would take her out of sight of the main hall, she glanced down to see her grandfather watching her, a slight frown on his face. As her eyes met his, he smiled swiftly and turned to enter a room to the left of the hall. She felt a sudden fear. Although he seemed pleased to have her here, was she in some way causing him to frown worriedly?

Lavinia promised herself solemnly that she would devote herself entirely to obeying her grandfather's every command, and in so doing she would attempt with every day to repay the debt of gratitude she owed him.

Perhaps, if she concentrated hard enough on other people and other things, she would not find Jonathan so much in her thoughts.

The days and weeks passed, winter gave way to early spring, and Lavinia grew more contented with each passing hour. She enjoyed wandering through the vast number of rooms at 'Avonridge'. The long drawing-room had windows down one side, the huge marble fireplace being on the opposite wall. The furniture—chosen with her grandmother's influence Lavinia imagined—was in the French style, the chairs and small side tables with graceful lines and gently curving legs, and the chairs upholstered in rich brocade or tapestries which, she learnt later, her grandmother had worked. Various portraits lined the walls—ancestors, she presumed. The one immediately above the fireplace intrigued her. The gentle face held some resemblance to herself, Lavinia could see, but the woman in the portrait. Lady Rowan, was beautiful and elegant and the girl who stared up at it with soulful brown eyes envied the face on the canvas.

Lavinia's favourite room was the library: its high ceiling with pictures painted on it: the walls lined with books and the comfortable couch where she would curl up with a book and lose herself among its pages forgetting for a time the world of reality.

Lavinia was happier at 'Avonridge' than she had ever been in her life and only one thing was missing to complete her happiness, but at the beginning of May even that was to be remedied, it seemed, for least for an all-too-short weekend.

The Eldon family were coming to stay at 'Avonridge'.

Lavinia's joy at the thought of seeing Jonathan once more was, however, tinged with fear and dread. She felt so gauche and awkward with him. How she wished she could see him but not be seen by him—but such a thought was ridiculous.

The time since she had come to 'Avonridge' had been the happiest she had ever known. In the company of her grandfather, she had blossomed into a normal, healthy young girl—still very shy, still lacking self-confidence, but her new-found happiness was reflected in her gentle smile and even her brown eyes had lost some of their sadness. Lord Rowan found that Lavinia—though her education had been sadly neglected as she herself had told him—had, nevertheless, a lively and active mind and under his guidance her general education improved rapidly. He himself gave her lessons each morning, and during the afternoon they drove or walked or occasionally rode, though the latter could be considered 'lessons' at first, for Lavinia knew not even the rudiments of horsemanship. However, Lord Rowan found her a willing and able pupil, though, unknown to him, her eagerness stemmed from her desire to become a person more worthy of Jonathan's notice. Whilst she could never seriously think that he could fall in love with her, still there was the unquenchable wish within her to become the sort of woman he would not be ashamed to accompany. Always in her mind's eye floated the picture of the beautiful Lady Anthea Thorwald whom Giles said Jonathan had once loved.

During Lavinia's moments of solitude, when Lord Rowan was engaged in business, she would return to her favourite pastime of sketching. Her grandfather knew of this interest, but she had never, even yet, dared to show him her efforts. Lavinia herself, considered them of little importance or interest to anyone else, though she gained much pleasure from the execution of her little pictures. She kept her work in a green folder, but she never felt the need to hide the folder as she had done in her parents' house, safe in the knowledge that her grandfather respected her need and wish for privacy in this respect. He would not, she knew, look upon her work unless she herself desired him to do so.

Increasingly often, she found herself sketching Jonathan. She drew his face from all angles—so well had she absorbed every expression of the face she loved. Occasionally she drew Giles, Lady Melmoth, Lord Melmoth and her grandfather.

Never did she recall the faces of her parents or brother on paper.

Only the faces of people she loved had she committed to memory so perfectly as to be able to reproduce them from memory: and the face her pencil sketched the most was Jonathan's.

On the day the Eldons were expected, Lord Rowan said at breakfast.

'No lessons today, my dear. I have some business to attend to before Melmoth arrives. Amuse yourself but don't stray far from the house.'

'No, Grandfather. What time will I . . . will they be here?'

'Late afternoon, I should think, in good time for dinner.'

The day was sunny and warm for early May. The garden was peaceful, save for the twittering and singing of birds. Lavinia was seated on a white-painted garden seat near a pool in the centre of which was a fountain springing from an urn held by a white marble figure—a woman of ancient times carrying the urn on her shoulder.

The fountain cascaded in silver drops all round the figure into the round pool below, the borders of which were covered with water-lilies, and if she bent forward, Lavinia could see goldfish darting to and fro beneath the dark green circular leaves of the lilies. The fountain—Lavinia's favourite spot—was in a small enclosed garden which she learnt from Mrs Matthews, had been her grandmother's favourite spot too. It seemed natural for the lonely child to find herself drawn to this place, drawn to the garden beloved by the woman who, had she lived, would have loved Lavinia too.

When Lord Rowan had for the first time found Lavinia seated in exactly the same place as his wife had so often sat, the pain of remembrance was sharp, and yet at the same moment he was filled with a quiet happiness at seeing the young girl growing towards the woman her grandmother had been, even to finding affinity with her in her garden.

The garden was situated at the back and some distance away from the house and so Lavinia did not hear the carriage and did not know of the Eldons' arrival until Giles' voice broke into her day-dreaming.

'Why, there you are, Vinny, hiding yourself away. Come and greet your guests.'

'Oh!' She jumped up, startled from her reverie. The folder of sketches slipped to the ground, scattering the papers on to the slabbed pathway round the pool.

'Careful,' cried Giles hurrying forward. 'You'll lose your papers in the water.'

He bent to help her gather the sheets of paper together.

'It's all right—really,' she said in confusion and fear that he would see the drawings.

'Hey, Vinny. These are marvellous. Why, there's one of Jonathan. My, my, that's wonderful—so lifelike. And here's one of Papa and Mama together. Vinny, you've talent, great talent. Here's one of me. Ha-ha,' he laughed delightedly to see his beaming face staring back at him from the paper. 'And another of old Jonathan, and another, and another, and . . .'

'Please, Giles, give them back to me.'

He looked up then from the pictures and saw her face suffused with hot embarrassment.

'Why, Vinny, don't be shy of *these*. They're superb. You shouldn't be hiding all this away. We must show the others.'

'No—no, Giles. I beg you,' she cried in anguished tones.

'But why ever not?'

'I'd rather you d-didn't. Even Grandfather—he's never seen my sketches. I prefer no one to see them.'

'But Vinny, why? These should be framed and hanging on a wall.

You should be provided with paints and try portraiture in oils—really you should. These of old Jonathan are really something, it's as if you . . .'

He stopped and regarded her closely. She avoided his penetrating gaze.

'Please give them back to me,' she said in a low voice.

'Vinny, tell me something,' Giles said in his impetuous way. 'Have you fallen for old Jonathan?'

'I—no, no of course not,' she said swiftly—too swiftly—her colour rising again.

'You're not a very good liar, Vinny dear,' Giles said softly.

'Giles Eldon—how dare you call me a l-liar,' she said, near to tears.

'There, there, Vinny. I promise your secret is safe with me. Both the drawings and Jonathan.'

'Giles—oh Giles,' her voice broke on a sob. 'Don't tell him, don't *ever* tell him. He'd hate me.'

'Never, Vinny, he could never do that. Come now, dry your tears.'

'But do you promise?' she asked earnestly.

'Yes—yes, I promise. Poor Vinny, you do have some bad luck. Now why,' he continued in a lighter, teasing vein, trying to win a smile back to her face, 'didn't you fall in love with a handsome chap like me?—I'm really quite jealous.'

'Oh Giles—I do l-love you,' she blushed even more at her boldness, 'but . . .'

'But you love Jonathan more and *not* as a brother, eh?'

She nodded.

Giles sighed. He could never be anything but completely honest, and he could not, therefore, lie now to Lavinia, not even to give her hope as so many would have done, for he knew it would be a false hope.

'Vinny, try to forget him. He doesn't seem to be the marrying kind—now, and . . .'

'Oh Giles, I know he'd never want to marry me. Good heavens after loving Lady Anthea . . .' Her voice faded into silence and though Giles gave her a look of complete and sympathetic understanding, and tucked her small hand in his arm, he could not, in truth, disagree with her.

They returned to the house and were there greeted by the rest of the Eldon family—Lady Melmoth with her charming smile, Lord Melmoth with his robust chuckle and Jonathan with his quiet, half-smile and brown eyes which regarded Lavinia so steadily, making her heart pound and her hands tremble.

Giles, true to his word, put the folder of drawings on a side table and made no further reference to it, but immediately complimented Lord Rowan on the appearance of the grounds.

'Really, sir, I thought there was no finer place than our own country house, but I begin to have doubts. 'Avonbridge' looks better than ever.'

The family laughed. There was one thing about Giles, Lavinia thought fondly, his readiness to defend anyone not only led him into trouble but also led him to perform acts of kindness, such as at this moment, when she knew he was deliberately drawing the attention away from her to himself in an effort to help her combat her shyness.

The Eldons' visit was all too short. The following morning the gentlemen went riding and although they invited Lavinia to accompany them—and she would dearly have loved to have gone so that she might be a little longer in Jonathan's company—she had to decline for her riding ability she knew was not proficient enough to enable her to keep pace with their speed. Nevertheless, she spent a pleasant morning with Lady Melmoth.

'Lavinia, my dear, you look so much happier. Do you like it here?'

'Oh so much, Lady Melmoth. I'm so grateful to you for all you did in bringing my grandfather and me together.'

'Nonsense, dear child. We were only too glad to be of some use. But Lavinia, whilst we have a moment to ourselves, I want a quiet talk with you. It may be none of my business, but knowing your grandfather would never discuss such matters with you—well—I think you should know.'

'Know what, Lady Melmoth?'

The good lady sighed. 'Your father has caused your grandfather a great deal of unhappiness in the past.'

'Oh, I can guess he has, for they have been estranged for years—and I can see now that it could not have been Grandfather's fault.'

'Quite so. But you are now making up for all his past unhappiness. Lord Rowan loves you dearly and you will be a great comfort to him.'

'I'll try, r-really I will.'

'Of course you will, child. But I think you should be warned. Your father may try to use you for his own ends, he may try to get you to intercede for him with your grandfather.'

The girl nodded, understanding quickly.

'But,' Lady Melmoth continued, 'you should have nothing to do with them, your father, your mother, or your brother.'

Lavinia looked surprised, but not shocked.

'I know this is a terrible thing to be telling a young girl, but Lord Melmoth and Jonathan have now found beyond doubt that your father and your brother are still engaged in business with Lord Thorwald and Lord Myron, who, as you know, are rivals of the Keldon Line—and such rivals who would stop at nothing, absolutely *nothings* to put the Keldon Line out of business and rain us. Do you understand, Lavinia?'

She nodded again.

'So it would be wiser if you severed all connections with the rest of your family, as indeed your grandfather has done. You don't *mind*, do you?'

'No—no. In time I would probably have forgiven them for their treatment of me, but if they are working against Grandfather and Lord Melmoth and—and J-Jonathan, then I can see you are right.'

'It goes against my nature, I must admit,' sighed Lady Melmoth, 'to preach non-forgiveness. I have always believed that life is too short to quarrel, especially with one's family, but your parents have been given more than one chance to rectify the mistakes they have made and be reconciled with your grandfather—but their treatment of you, my dear, has put an end to any possibility of reconciliation in the future, I know.'

'Why did they invite you to dine and at the same time send me to Lord Myron?'

Lady Melmoth glanced at the girl shrewdly. Lavinia was not the simpleton one could have once supposed when they had first met her.

'Ah—now this is getting a little involved with business intrigue, my dear. If I tell you, you must promise never to tell anyone for it could have serious repercussions upon your grandfather and on all of us.'

'Of course, I won't say a word,' Lavinia breathed.

'You know of Jonathan's steamship?'

'Yes.'

Lady Melmoth smiled. 'We call it "Jonathan's" although, of course, it is the Company's but he centres all his hopes upon it. He says it is the ship of the future, that one day the clipper ships—dependent upon the elements as they are—will be obsolete eventually.'

'I understand, but why should Lord Thorwald be opposed to it?'

'They don't believe in steam, neither do they have the capital, from what we hear, to risk building a steamship which after all might be a failure. It has not been proved yet.'

'But if Jonathan believes in it, then it must be all right.'

Lady Melmoth smiled at the implicit faith Lavinia placed in Jonathan.

'Well, we all hope so, naturally.'

'But I still don't see . . .'

'Thorwald and Myron, as I said, would stop at nothing. We fear they may try sabotage of the ship or other ways to discredit our name and harm our Company. And as your father is now involved with them, we think he invited us to dine to try and join the Keldon Line so that, if he was allowed to do so, he could then relay confidential information to Thorwald and Myron.'

The girl was silent for a moment as if unable to comprehend such a startling piece of knowledge about her own father.

'I understand,' she said quietly, at last.

The matter was not referred to again, but Lavinia thought of their conversation often and worried for Jonathan's safety.

During the Eldons' stay at 'Avonbridge' Lavinia never once found herself alone with Jonathan and after they had left she could not decide whether she was pleased or sorry, for whilst it would have been a pleasure, at the same time she would have been fearful of appearing foolish in his eyes because of her shyness.

He had, of course, exchanged the usual idle conversation with her, but always during the presence of another member of the family. So Lavinia watched their carriage depart with sadness and wondered how long it would be before she would see Jonathan—or any of them—again.

'Come and sit down, my child,' Lord Rowan said. 'I have something to tell you.'

Lavinia took one last glance at the disappearing carriage and turned from the window.

'I have been talking with Lord and Lady Melmoth this week-end, and asking their advice about you.'

'About m-me?'

'Yes. You see, my dear, I cannot teach you all a young lady of your position ought to know.'

'M-my position?'

'Yes—you see I shall make you my sole heiress. You will one day be a lady of considerable standing and make a good marriage. But to do all this you must be educated properly. I could, of course, get a governess for you, but that would not give you a wider knowledge. You ought to travel, to see a bit of the world before you settle down with a husband and family.'

Lavinia did not know what her grandfather's conversation was leading up to but she feared it all the same.

'So I think you should go away to school for a year.'

'G-go away,' her voice was little more than a whisper.

'Lavinia, I don't want you to go—I'll miss you more than I can say,' he took her hands in his and looked into hers. 'But it is for your own sake, do you understand?'

Dully, she nodded. Though her heart was breaking, she would have to do as her grandfather wished.

'We think the best place is a finishing school in France.'

'*Abroad!*' She looked up, startled to retort. 'So *far* away?'

'France was your grandmother's county. I want you to learn something of her people and nowhere else in the world will you learn the intricacies of social etiquette any better.'

'A whole year away in France,' she whispered.

'It will soon go. Believe me, child, it will be far longer for me than for you.'

But Lavinia could not agree. A year away from Jonathan. A year in which so much could happen. He could be married by the time she returned.

Lavinia felt her heart breaking over Jonathan for the second time, even though this time he was not directly the cause of it.

Chapter Six

The arrangements for Lavinia's departure for France were completed, it seemed to Lavinia, with frightening swiftness. She was to start at the school in September and the following weeks seemed to disappear and it was August before she realised it. Much to her chagrin she found she would have to leave without seeing the Eldons again, and although Lady Melmoth wrote her a kind letter of affectionate good wishes and Giles penned a scribbled note, no word came from Jonathan. Not that she expected it, but she had hoped that in some way she might see him again—just once more—before she went away for a whole year. Naturally, too, she would miss her grandfather of whom she was very fond, and the other three members of the Eldon family, but it was Jonathan who remained uppermost in her thoughts.

As the day of her departure grew nearer. Lord Rowan spent more and more time with Lavinia, and any fears she may have had that she was being sent away because she was an encumbrance upon him were dispelled. So obvious was his dismay at the thought of being parted from her so soon after having found her, that Lavinia, for a time, forgot her own sadness in trying to erase, or at least ease, his.

The morning of their embarkation at Dover found them at the harbour early, having stayed overnight in an hotel nearby. The quay was a seething mass of people scurrying hither and thither intent upon their own affairs. Lavinia was bewildered and a little frightened by it all. Although she was a city girl, she had never seen such a throng. She held on tightly to her grandfather's arm, afraid that she would lose him in the crowd.

'There they are,' a voice cried close at hand and Lavinia turned to see Giles pushing his way through the people to reach them, and following in his wake was Jonathan.

'Couldn't let you go without saying a proper "goodbye", Vinny. Good morning, Lord Rowan.' Giles was breathless.

'Good morning, my boy, Jonathan,' as the latter reached them.

Lavinia knew herself to be pink with the pleasure not only of actually seeing Jonathan but also with the thought that he had taken the trouble to come all this way to see her. Giles' next words were to dispel some of the magic of her thoughts.

'Jonathan had to come down here on business, so I decided to come with him and see you off.'

So Giles had come especially, Lavinia thought, but not Jonathan. However, she consoled herself, he had come, and she had had her wish to see him just once more granted. Giles chattered on in his usual boyishly impetuous manner, whilst Jonathan merely smiled down at her. At last Jonathan drew her aside from the other two for a brief moment and spoke softly to her alone.

'Don't be sad at going, Vinny. When you return you'll be an accomplished young lady with no reason to be shy or afraid of anyone.'

'You r-really think so?' Her eyes gazed into his appealingly, but her tone was disbelieving.

'You haven't any need now, although I know you won't believe me—but perhaps when you come back you will do so. Vinny, when you come back ...' his voice took on a note of urgency, but at that moment Giles called.

'It's time Vinny and Lord Rowan were going aboard, Jonathan.'

'All right,' he replied. 'Vinny—you will write to me—to us—and let us know how you are and ...'

'Yes—yes, I'll write and,' she paused uncertain whether she dare say what was in her mind.

'Yes?' he prompted.

'And I sh-should like to know h-how you—all—are, and about the clippers and your steamship.'

She saw the gleam of pleasure in his eyes at the mention of the steamship. Then he laughed. 'If I wrote to you on that subject, Vinny, I should bore you to tears.'

'Oh no—no—*you* c-could never do that,' she cried and then blushed and hung her head at the thought of her boldness.

'Really, Vinny,' Jonathan said so softly that she could scarcely hear him. 'I'm glad.'

'Hey, you two,' Giles broke in again. 'Come on, or you'll miss it.'

He appeared beside them and took Lavinia's hand and placed it through his arm. 'Allow me to escort you, ma'am.'

'Allow *me* to escort you, ma'am,' said Jonathan, his face breaking into one of his rare wide grins so that he looked almost as boyishly young as Giles. Only the scar was a sharp reminder that his youth had been somewhat carelessly misspent.

Lavinia took the arm Jonathan offered her and tried to laugh gaily, but the effort almost choked her with the thought that she would see neither of them for almost a year and so much could happen in that time.

As the boat drew away, Lord Rowan and Lavinia stood by the deck rail and waved to the two brothers until they were mere specks in the distance.

'They're fine young men, Lavinia, I should be more than happy if you eventually pick a husband who is their equal.'

Lavinia looked up to meet his eyes and knew by her expression that she betrayed herself if her grandfather could see it. She looked away quickly.

'Ah,' said Lord Rowan quietly. 'I seem to have struck upon a note which responds, have I, Lavinia?'

'Please, Grandfather, do not ask me.'

Tears were too close for her to discuss her feelings rationally at this moment and besides, she wanted no one else to learn of her hopeless love for Jonathan. It was bad enough that Giles should have learnt of it.

'Very well, my dear,' Lord Rowan put his arm about her shoulders and she leant against him. Together they watched the disappearing coast of England.

The school itself offered no fearful prospect of misery for the next year. It was a charming old house—rambling was the only word to describe it, Lavinia thought. A maze of corridors, classrooms, bedrooms and dormitories, and so on. The headmistress was a small woman, but exquisitely proportioned. Her serene face, still beautiful, was at one and the same time kindly and homely, but worldly-wise and intelligent. Madame Givelle was eminently suited to her profession.

'You are very welcome, Mamedolselle Kelvin,' she said, her English most beautifully pronounced with only the merest hint of an accent. 'Lord Rowan, I am happy to make your acquaintance. I am sure your grand-daughter will be happy here and you have my personal assurance that she will be well cared-for.'

'I am sure of that, Madame, for I selected your establishment only after very careful consideration and on the finest recommendation.'

Madame Givelle smiled and turned to Lavinia. 'Well, my dear, I will leave you to say "good-bye" to your grandfather. When you are ready, knock on my sitting-room door and we will have a little talk.' She waved her elegant hand to indicate the door of her room at one side of the vast hall in which they were now standing and then she left them.

'Now, my child, no painful "good-byes",' her grandfather said briskly. 'The time will soon pass and you will be back home with me.'

He kissed her on both cheeks.

'Au revoir,' he said softly, turned and walked away quickly before Lavinia had had time to utter a single word.

When the front door had closed behind his tall figure, she stood for a moment to swallow the lump in her throat and to wipe the tears from her eyes. Then, taking a deep breath to compose herself, she went and knocked upon Madame's door.

Life at Madame Givelle's finishing school was, at first, very strange for Lavinia. She had, whilst in her parents' household, never enjoyed much social life. She had never been allowed to make friends with girls of her own age, and so to be plunged into the midst of about thirty of forty young ladles, all of whom possessed an abundance of self-confidence which Lavinia did not, was in itself a challenge. But the whole atmosphere of the school was relaxed and friendly. To her surprise there were few strict rules and the members of staff were far from the stern taskmistresses she had anticipated they might be. As if following Madame's lead, they were kindly and sympathetic towards her and gave no indication that she was, at first, different from the rest of the pupils in their charge. It was not a school for academic learning only—though they had such lessons—but in the main the establishment was designed to equip girls of social standing with the graces and manners befitting their station, to give them self-confidence, charm and, in short, to make them worthy of a husband of high rank, for the thought uppermost in every girl's mind was of the husband she would one day hope to secure.

So Lavinia soon found herself reasonably happy in her new surroundings, and although she missed Jonathan, her grandfather and the Eldons intolerably, she comforted herself with the thought that when she returned she would be more the kind of woman whom Jonathan could admire. So she applied herself diligently to her lessons. Her favourite lesson was dancing—she loved the graceful steps to the music, learning the art of curtsying in the long, full skirts. Not so popular with any of the girls was the deportment class where they had to walk about with a heavy book upon their heads to acquire an elegant walk, and for the girl with a stoop there was the ordeal of spending some time each day strapped to a blackboard so that she might grow tall and straight. Fortunately, Lavinia had a natural grace and straightness of back which allowed her exemption from this. They learnt embroidery, making numerous fine samplers of different stitches and only when they could perform each stitch to perfection were they allowed to progress to the making of something more useful. The girls, too, were encouraged to paint, mostly in watercolours, and in this class Lavinia found she excelled. Soon her portraits of her fellow pupils were in great demand and before her year was out, she was to have painted almost every one of the inmates of the school—including Madame Givelle herself who, to Lavinia's great delight, insisted that her portrait should be framed and hung in her sitting-room. She was allowed to experiment with oils and found this medium even more to her liking. Lavinia found she enjoyed working with colours even more than with pencil and she also painted the faces of her grandfather and the Eldon family from memory—this time being careful however, to paint only one of Jonathan. But she could not help taking greater care over the portrait of Jonathan. There was no doubt that of all her work this stood out as her masterpiece. It was as if all her love for him transmitted itself through her brush on to the canvas. The portraits of her grandfather and of the Eldons she kept to take back with her—perhaps this time she would show them to her grandfather for Madame Givelle had complemented her on her talent and had told her that she must continue to work hard at her painting. The pencil drawings she had done previously—the ones Giles had come upon unexpectedly—had been left at home, but now she had a new set of drawings and paintings which were undoubtedly an improvement on her previous efforts now she had had encouragement and advice from the art mistress.

Lavinia also found, much to her surprise, that she enjoyed the learning of French. At first she had been distressed to find that she was the only pupil there who had not previously learnt anything of the language. But her quick mind soon rescued her from the bottom of the class, finding that she had perhaps a natural feeling for the language because it was her grandmother's tongue.

Letters arrived frequently from her grandfather, to which she replied with the same regularity. She also received letters from Lady Melmoth and Giles, but from Jonathan there was no word. She had been half-afraid that his promise to write had been just an idle one, as people do when they part. So that when a letter with strange handwriting arrived one day, she had ceased to hope that it might be from him, and when, on opening it, she saw the name 'Jonathan' at the foot of the page, she could scarcely believe it possible.

Without reading it she slipped it into the pocket of her morning dress for she had no wish to read it amongst the other girls who at any moment might peep over her shoulder. She would wait until she could slip away to the dormitory and read it in private. Some time later in the morning, after two hours of lessons on which she had found concentration difficult, her thoughts ever wandering to the letter in her pocket, she found herself running with undignified haste up the stairs to her room. With trembling fingers she sat down on the bed to read the letter, holding the page tenderly as if it were her most treasured possession.

'*My dear Lavinia,*

'*I trust this letter will find you as it leaves me—in good health. We have heard with pleasure from Lord Rowan of the comfort and suitability of your residence. I, for my part, hope you are happy in your present surroundings.*'

Lavinia could well imagine him pausing at this point to consider a topic on which he could write to make the letter of reasonable length, and falling back on the one subject which occupied the majority of his thoughts.

'*The steamship progresses favourably and we hope she will make her maiden voyage within a year or so. Rivalry grows between our Line and T & M. As you know the first clipper into the East India Docks in London with a new cargo of tea commands the higher prices and competition between the captains of the clippers of rival companies springs up automatically. Ships are now racing across the seas to be the first in port and folk here in London are even placing wagers as to which ship will be first home. Of course, other companies are involved too, but our greatest rivals are those afore-mentioned.*

'*Giles became involved (almost) in a brawl last week because someone dared to lay his wager against our line in favour of T & M.*'

The letter ended, rather abruptly, as if he had suddenly thought that Lavinia may not be interested in the only topic upon which Jonathan found he could write at length. It was strange that the quiet, reserved Jonathan could release such thoughts in a letter. Yet Lavinia, too, found herself in a similar position. It seemed that for both of them it was easier for them to put their thoughts down on paper, in the rather more impersonal form of a letter, than if they were conversing face to face. In her reply, Lavinia was somewhat surprised to find herself saying things to him she would never have dared to say directly to him.

'I am quite well settled here,' she wrote, 'and happy, but I do miss Grandfather and all of you so much.

'I am so glad the steamship progresses—will it be ready by the time the new canal opens? I would think that the first ships to make use of the much shorter route would reap the most benefit—and I remember you saying that clippers would be unable to use the canal.

'I can sympathise with Giles' feeling at hearing disparagement of our Line—but please tell him to take care, it will hardly help the Company if he gets himself harmed, even in its defence!'

She did not send her reply immediately for she did not wish to appear over-eager or to put Jonathan under an obligation to reply quickly to her letter. Of course, the words she would dearly loved to have penned remained unwritten and locked within her heart.

Lavinia was enraptured, however, to find that when she did at last send her letter, Jonathan replied almost by return.

'My dear Lavinia,

'Your letter delighted me and—forgive me—surprised me. The surprise was caused by your perceptive remark about the first ships through the canal. How right you are and (though you must keep this to yourself) our Company have this very fact in mind in building the steamship. We hope that the ship will be ready some months before the canal opens and can prove its seaworthiness and so on in good time so as to be running smoothly before the canal opens.'

Lavinia, once more anxious not to appear over-eager, purposely delayed her reply to Jonathan again, though during the following days the words of her proposed letter kept running through her mind. When she did reply, she made her letter lengthy telling him of her life at the school, of the kindness of her teachers and of the friendliness of the girls. One girl in particular, another English girl, Phillippa Selwyn, had become Lavinia's particular companion. They shared a room together and the girl, vivacious and charming, had taken the shy Lavinia under her protective wing. Lavinia admired her greatly. She wrote to Jonathan of her.

'*Lady Phillippa Selwyn is so gay and attractive and so self-confident—how I admire her! She is kind too. She comes from London, though I'm not sure what part, and her family have a country house in Devon, I believe.*'

It was a long time before Jonathan wrote again—all of six weeks and Lavinia, though she had at first been overwhelmed by the speed with which he had answered her first letter, now found herself deeply disappointed that he should take such a long time to write again. She wondered whether she could have offended him in some way and though she recalled to mind almost every word of her letter to him, she could think of nothing to which Jonathan could or would have taken exception.

A letter arrived from Giles and his words regarding Jonathan perplexed Lavinia more than ever.

'*Old Jonathan has been like a grumpy bear these last weeks—goodness knows what's the matter with him.*'

The remainder of Giles' letter was general chatter telling her of various balls and social functions he had attended. He had been to the music-hall, he told her, and had enjoyed it immensely.

'*I can't drag old Jonathan along though—he seems to have no taste for the high life now. He just wants to bury himself in work and his steamship.'*

At last, a letter arrived from Jonathan and once more Lavinia took it to the privacy of her bedroom before opening it. She was half-afraid to read it, fearful that he was in some way angry with her from what Giles had told her. But his letter gave no indication that he was in any way put out and he only apologised briefly for not having written before, but explained that pressure of business had kept him occupied.

Perhaps, she thought, the final paragraph held the only clue—if there was one—as to the reason for his ill-temper of which Giles had spoken.

'I am happy,' Jonathan wrote, *'to hear you are making friends, but take care to whom you give your friendship, my dear. Not everyone is what they seem.'*

Here he started to write more, but the word was heavily scored through and Lavinia was left wondering what he had been about to write. She sat on the edge of her bed in the silence of the room, the only sounds being the muted voices of the other girls from downstairs. Lavinia wrinkled her brow. Jonathan seemed to be warning her against false friendliness shown to her by the inmates of the school. But, as she recalled, the only person to whom she had alluded in her letter to him had been Phillippa Selwyn.

Selwyn! Where had she heard the name before? Now she came to think about it, when she had first learnt it was Phillippa's family name, it had struck a chord of recognition somewhere, but until this moment she had thought no more of it.

Lavinia shook her head slowly. She knew now that she had definitely heard mention of the name before, but she could not recall when or from whom.

She locked the precious letter from Jonathan in the drawer of her bedside table. She smoothed her hair back from her forehead and regarded herself in the looking-glass. Already, there were distinct changes in her appearance since she had left England. She had lost her pallor and her complexion was now smooth and glowing. Her figure, once so childish for her age, was now softly blossoming into young womanhood, though her naturally tiny waist was the envy of many of the plumper girls in the school who laced themselves ever tighter to assimilate Lavinia's slender proportions. She had learnt to dress her hair into various fashionable styles, for, although she would no doubt have her own personal maid when she returned to 'Avonridge', as Madame said, 'We do not want to be at the mercy of a maid for the elegance of our appearance, do we?'

But still the brown eyes staring back at her were filled with a sadness not easily understood by others. She sighed and turned away. Superficially, she was happy enough here, but as with each passing day she grew towards womanhood, so the love in her heart for Jonathan changed from girlish adoration or infatuation, into a deep and lasting emotion, whether or not it would or could ever be returned by him.

Lavinia decided to make little of her life at the school in her future letters to Jonathan, hardly mentioning her friend, Phillippa. She pressed him for more details of his ship, which course was wise on her part, for no other subject could tempt such lengthy letters from the reserved Jonathan. He referred, often, but always guardedly, to the increasing antagonism between the Keldon Line and their rivals who, though Jonathan avoided actually writing their names in full in his letters, Lavinia knew to be the Line run by Lord Myron and Lord Thorwald in which her own father was also engaged. As the building of the steamship progressed, Lavinia heard of the strict security measures her grandfather, Lord Melmoth and his two sons were taking to safeguard their ship. Why, wondered Lavinia, pausing in reading a letter from Jonathan, should it be necessary to have a guard patrolling day and night near the ship?

A week later, a letter from Giles gave her the answer, and at the same time taught her several things, not only about the seriousness of the rivalry between the Companies, but also about Jonathan himself.

'*Dear Vinny,*' Giles wrote.

'*Jonathan has asked me to write to you—though I was on the point of doing so on my own account. He has had to rush off to Blackwall as we've run into a spot of bother. I believe you know that rivalry between our two Companies has grown, and their antagonism is directed towards our new ship. Well, as a security we have been guarding her, but honestly, I don't think any of us thought they would stoop to this! Vinny, the new ship has been sabotaged. Fortunately no one was hurt, but the ship is badly damaged and it will take weeks or months probably, to repair. So you can guess how we're all feeling here. Jonathan has gone there and I think he plans to stay on the spot at least until things have quietened down.*'

Lavinia paused. So Jonathan has rushed off immediately to guard his beloved ship with no thought for his own personal safety. And it had also meant that he was too busy to write to her and had asked Giles to do so instead. Lavinia sighed. How many times did Jonathan—unwittingly—break her heart?

Chapter Seven

It was eight weeks and three days after Giles' letter telling her of the sabotage to the steamship before Lavinia received a hastily scribbled note from Jonathan.

'*My dear Vinny,*' She was surprised to see this instead of Lavinia.

'*Forgive me, my dear, for not having written and for having asked Giles to write to you in my stead. I hope you will understand the desperate urgency of the situation in which we found ourselves at that time. I know Giles will have acquainted you with as much detail as he was able to put in a letter—and you will no doubt also have heard further from your grandfather—so now, suffice to say that although the ship was badly damaged we have been able to repair it and are now proceeding with the normal building, though some months behind schedule. But this is not a serious problem. The only real worry now is the possibility of a re-occurrence of the sabotage. But all we can do is to take every precaution and hope nothing more will happen.*

'*We have another problem, Vinny, with which perhaps you can help us. We want a name for our brand new ship. We had thought of the "Mélanie" after your grandmother, but how do you feel about us calling her the "Lavinia"? All the family—including your grandfather—are in full agreement with my suggestion, and all we need now is your approval.*'

Lavinia could for the moment read no further for tears of joy blinded her. Jonathan did think enough of her to wish to name his new ship—for she had always thought of it as his—after her. It was strange, she reflected later when her emotions had calmed somewhat, that such little actions by Jonathan could either cast her into the depths of despair or elevate her to the clouds. Such was the penalty of loving!

Naturally, she replied immediately to him this time, but because she was so overwhelmed by his gesture, her letter was perhaps a little stilted in her acceptance. She could not put into words all that it meant to her, and of course, it was necessary to hide from him just exactly how much his action did mean to her.

The year of her stay in France was fast nearing conclusion and only two months remained before she would be sailing home. Her grandfather wrote—as he had done each week since their parting—and spoke of her homecoming.

'We are planning to give you a grand "coming-out" ball, my dear, and Lady Melmoth will present you at Court and attend to all the engagements which you will have in your first Season. Now, about your journey from France—will you mind if I don't make the journey to fetch you, my dear? The injury to my leg—I told you I had a fall whilst riding—is still rather painful though nothing serious I assure you, but the long journey would not help. Giles has expressed a great willingness to come over and escort you back to England, for I would not dream of having you travel alone. He really is a most likeable young man—impetuous perhaps, but completely trustworthy. I know he will take good care of you.'

Lavinia frowned. Was her grandfather's injury more serious than he had hitherto led her to believe? He had made light of the mishap when it had occurred—but now she began to worry about him. She could not, despite her anxiety, help smiling at his words regarding Giles. She remembered their conversation on the boat when she had left England when her grandfather had seen her unhappiness at leaving the Eldon brothers. She wondered now whether he thought that Giles was the object of her affection.

As far as Lord Rowan's injury was concerned, she did not know what to do; she could not write and ask him for he would dismiss it entirely, and though she would see him for herself in less than two months that was still a long time to be worrying.

Lavinia decided to write to Lady Melmoth for she better than the menfolk of the family would understand the disquiet in Lavinia's mind. But her fears were quelled by the reply which assured her that Lady Melmoth was convinced that Lord Rowan's injury was not in the least serious—but that he was taking the wise precaution of nursing it.

> '*I am sure,*' Lady Melmoth wrote in conclusion, '*that the injury has certainly caused him a deal of pain, but by his appearance I can tell that it is improving steadily now, though perhaps at the time it happened he did minimise the accident to you!*'

So Lavinia began to look forward to her home-going with uninterrupted pleasure. She had acquired a large—she still wondered at times if it were not too large—wardrobe of fashionably elegant clothes. Her whole appearance was altered beyond even her own hopes. She had acquired too the elegance and self-confidence she had once so envied in Lady Melmoth and indeed also in Lady Anthea Thorwald.

Always foremost in her mind was the question—what would Jonathan think of her now?

One month: three weeks: two: one—and then the day was here! There was a mixture of happiness and sadness for all the girls were excited at the prospect of returning home and yet having lived together for almost a year, it was natural that friendships had been formed and parting brought the inevitable 'sweet sorrow'.

Madame Givelle was high in the girls' affections and Lavinia in particular felt a deep gratitude to the kindly woman for, of all the girls, Lavinia knew she had learned the most and gained the most benefit under Madame's guidance. In her wildest dreams she had never really anticipated that she could emerge the self-assured, elegant woman she now was.

Lavinia dressed with care on the morning of her departure. Her travelling habit was new, the skirt following the latest trend in fashion, being less of the full-skirted crinoline, but flatter in the front and falling to a train. Over this she wore a tight-fitting short coat for it was July and very warm. The coat was royal blue velvet and she wore a matching hat trimmed with white silk ribbons, feathers and artificial flowers. Her hair was drawn back from her face in waves into a cascade of ringlets at the back of her head.

Lavinia and her friend Phillippa, ready at last, found themselves standing on the steps at the front of the house, awaiting the arrival of Giles and Phillippa's brother who was coming to escort her home.

'I hope you will like my brother, Lavinia,' Phillippa Selwyn remarked as they reached the driveway. 'I am sure he will fall in love with you at once.'

Lavinia laughed. She had told no one, not even Phillippa, of her affection for Jonathan and so that no one would suspect she had always indulged in the chatter of 'match-making'.

'I am sure, Phillippa, that with all the other girls here, he will never notice me. He will be mesmerised with so many eligible females at once.'

'Ah, but don't forget we are to travel to England together. You'll have plenty of time to ensnare him with your charms, whilst I shall enslave Giles Eldon.'

'Oh no—if anyone is going to enslave Giles, it will be me—I have prior claim, don't forget,' Lavinia teased her friend.

'Then that leaves me with no one,' Phillippa replied, pretending to pout. 'Are you really attracted to Giles, Lavinia, you've not said?'

'He's very kind and very good-looking,' she replied guardedly. 'But shall we say more of a brother to me.'

'There you are then,' Phillippa waved her slender hand, 'you don't want him yourself, but you won't let *me* have him. Really, Lavinia, you're . . .'

But her remonstrations were cut short as Lavinia interrupted her friend with a cry of delight.

'Here's Giles,' and as a carriage drew to a halt, she hurried forward to meet the tall figure stepping down from it.

'Giles! Giles!'

The young man looked around and his eyes came to rest upon the girl hurrying towards him. Lavinia saw the puzzlement on his face turn to surprised wonderment.

'Vinny—Vinny, is it really you?'

As he took her outstretched hands in his, she laughed delightedly, but could not resist teasing him.

'Giles—have you forgotten me in only a year? Shame on you—you wound me, sir!'

'Forget you! Never, Vinny, but you've changed so—grown up. You're lovely— beautiful'

'Nonsense, Giles,' she laughed.

'It is not nonsense,' he murmured, continuing to gaze at her as if he could not believe the picture before his eyes.

'Good grief,' he exclaimed as he began to recover from his surprise, which Lavinia realised was genuine, 'it hardly seems possible—just wait till old Jonathan sees you!'

The smile faded a little from her face as Giles touched upon the subject closest to her heart—even she dared not put into words the hopes she cherished.

'Come,' she said putting her hand on his arm, 'and meet my dear friend, Phillippa Selwyn.'

Lavinia noticed the startled look in his eyes, but he remained silent as she led him forward to meet her friend. The formal introductions over, there was an awkward pause. Giles seemed ill-at-ease and unwilling to meet Phillippa's eyes, although he answered her questions politely enough.

'Did you have a good journey, Mr Eldon?'

'Yes, Lady Phillippa, I thank you.'

Another pause.

'I understand we are to travel back together—the four of us,' she continued.

'Four?' Now he looked at her questioningly.

'Why yes, my brother, Francis too. He should be here any moment.'

Giles stiffened visibly and could not hide a fleeting frown.

'Why, Mr Eldon, are you not agreeable to the arrangement? Do you *know* my brother?'

'I . . .'

Giles was, however, saved the embarrassment of answering her direct question, for at that moment the subject of thier conversation approached.

'Phillippa.'

'Francis—at last, I thought you had forgotten to come.'

They greeted each other casually with none of the affection which had been underlying the greeting between Giles and Lavinia.

Phillippa made the introductions.

Lord Francis took Lavinia's hand in his, kissed the tips of her fingers and gazed into her eyes.

'Enchanting,' he murmured.

Lavinia smiled politely but she was not taken in by what she was sure was flattery.

As Phillippa introduced Giles, the two men eyed each other warily.

'So, the *younger* Eldon, eh?' Lord Francis Selwyn raised a quizzical eyebrow. 'We've never met, but no doubt you've heard of me, eh?' He laughed.

'I have,' replied Giles shortly. 'Good morning, Lady Phillippa. Come Lavinia . . .'

'But Giles . . .' she glanced helplessly at Phillippa who seemed as puzzled as Lavinia.

As they moved out of earshot, Lavinia said, 'Really, Giles, that was uncommonly rude of you—how can you be so discourteous to my friend, even if you do not like her brother, which is obvious?'

Giles said nothing, but she noticed that he was breathing heavily and his lips were pursed with suppressed anger.

'Giles—what is all this about?'

'Vinny—you still care for Jonathan, don't you?'

She gasped. 'You have—it's not fair to ask me such a question.'

'Very well. But if you do you'll keep away from the Selwyns.'

'Why?' Lavinia's eyes were wide in astonishment.

'Because—because Selwyn is the man Jonathan is supposed to have fought a duel with—over Lady Anthea. It was Selwyn who gave him that scar.'

'Oh no!' Lavinia's reply was but a whisper.

'Yes,' continued Giles bitterly. 'It must have caused him a great deal of unhappiness at the time—and because of Selwyn, he bears a scar which will never allow him to forget.'

Lavinia was thoughtful. Now she understood the reason for the strangeness in Jonathan's letter after she had mentioned her friendship with Lady Phillippa Selwyn. They walked over the lawn in silence. At last she said slowly,

'I don't believe Jonathan is the sort to bear malice after all this time—and even if he is, his bitterness cannot extend to Lord Selwyn's sister and it is her with whom I am friendly, not Lord Francis.'

'But she's *his* sister—a close relation.'

Lavinia withdrew her hand from his arm abruptly and turned to face him.

'Do you class all members of a family together, Giles? Do you blame *me* for what my father and brother have done?'

'Vinny, Vinny,' he said placatingly, his anger dying as hers grew. 'That's different.'

'Of course it isn't. Phillippa cannot be held responsible for what her brother did years ago, any more than I can help what my father has done.'

'Vinny—I'm sorry—truly I am. You're right, of course.' He smiled ruefully. '*You* may have grown up, little Vinny, but it seems that I am as hot-headed as ever.'

Lavinia smiled, her anger forgotten now beneath his boyish admission of impetuosity. Perhaps she had grown up quickly, she thought, in an effort to bridge the gap of years which lay between her and Jonathan.

Lavinia was able to explain away the incident to her friend without giving away the truth.

'Some family quarrel ages ago, Phil, let's take no notice if they want to be silly.'

So the two girls agreed to ignore the coolness between the two gentlemen on the journey home. Nevertheless, Lavinia, despite her affection for her friend Phillippa, could not find it in herself to like Lord Francis, Viscount Selwyn. He was handsome, there was no disputing that. But his mouth was small and cruel and his eyes hard. He was slim and straight—like Jonathan—but with a rigidity born of conceit. His face wore a perpetual disdainful expression as though all his fellow creatures bored him. But, if he wished, Lord Francis could exert a charm not easily surpassed. A pretty compliment was ever ready on his lips and his attentiveness towards Lavinia was only interrupted by Giles' presence.

Phillippa, finding that some feud existed between her brother and the attractive Giles, shrugged her shoulders philosophically and decided not to try to indulge in a mild flirtation with him. For one thing, she might well suffer the embarrassment of a rebuff for Giles, despite Lavinia's protestations, could not bring himself to act naturally towards Lady Phillippa, and secondly, her brother would be sure to frown upon it. So she would concentrate upon her arrival in London, which city she planned to take by storm. At least she would do so, she mused, if Lavinia were not such an obvious rival. Her friend was an undoubted rival for the eligible bachelors of Society. Fortunately, there was no jealousy in Phillippa's nature and she was generous enough to wish for her friend's success as much as her own.

Their arrival at Dover was greeted by waiting relations, for there were several other girls travelling back to England, together with other passengers from France. From the deck, Giles seemed to be scanning the crowd below anxiously.

'Whom are you looking for?' Lavinia asked.

'I thought perhaps—never mind, no—there he is—I *thought* he'd come,' he said delightedly.

'Who—who, Grandfather?' she cried.

'No, no, Jonathan, of course.'

'*Jonathan!* Here. Jonathan here? Oh where?'

'There—see, over there.'

Lavinia followed his pointing finger and indeed, alone at the back of the waiting crowd was Jonathan, standing patiently until they could join him. Giles waved and after a few moments, Jonathan saw them and returned the wave. Lavinia, her heart pounding foolishly, fluttered her hand briefly in greeting, but only once for she did not wish to appear over-eager.

'I *knew* he'd come,' Giles repeated. 'I know he's so busy just now with the ship nearing launching, but I thought he wouldn't let me—you down.'

Lavinia was quick to hear the slip of his tongue.

'You, Giles? Let *you* down? Giles, did you ask him to meet us?'

'No—of course I—er—um,' he subsided in embarrassment. 'Well, I did just say—but he was coming anyway, really he was.'

The joy of seeing Jonathan waiting on the landing stage was diminished now for he had not come at his own wish but at Giles' insistence.

'Giles,' she said in sudden alarm, 'you've never—told him, you wouldn't betray my trust, would you?'

'No, Vinny, I wouldn't do that. Maybe I am always putting my foot in it—I have just now—but I don't break a confidence like that.'

She smiled. 'Thank you, Giles.'

Lavinia and Phillippa took their leave of each other before disembarkation. It was obvious that Giles and Francis did not wish to prolong each other's company and when Francis heard that Jonathan awaited them he was as anxious as Giles that they should part company. With promises to correspond and to meet again at a later date, the two girls separated, Phillippa to try her hand in the marriage-market and Lavinia to meet again the family she loved so dearly—and one person in particular.

As he came towards them, she saw Jonathan had not changed at all and now the long months were behind her it seemed but yesterday since she had seen him.

But there was a change—not in him but in her and she could read in his eyes that he saw it immediately. She was no longer a shy, awkward girl, but a woman—Giles had said beautiful. In Jonathan's eyes as they met she saw first joy, then surprise swiftly followed by a strange look of hopelessness which she found hard to understand.

'My dear Vinny,' he said softly as he took her hands.

'Jonathan,' was all she found she could say for the lump in her throat. Her eyes filled with tears as he kissed her cheek in a brotherly manner.

Then the two brothers one on either side each took her arm.

'Who would have thought, Giles, that this is the same little girl we rescued that night?' Jonathan smiled that strange half-smile as he looked down at her.

'I almost didn't know her,' Giles said. Jonathan's smile broadened.

'She couldn't change so much for me—I knew she'd be beautiful one day.'

Lavinia blushed.

'Now we're embarrassing her—besides, you'll make her conceited,' Giles admonished his brother playfully. 'It's not only her appearance that's changed—she's already put me in my place.'

'Really,' Jonthan raised his eyebrows. 'I thought we could trust you, Giles?'

'Oh not like that—dash it all,' Giles said quickly. 'You tell him, Vinny.'

'You remember me telling you in a letter, Jonathan, of my friendship with Lady Phillippa Selwyn?'

She thought a look of pain crossed his face but he replied steadily enough, 'Yes.'

'Well, at the time I thought your reply—your warning almost—a little strange, but now I understand.'

Jonathan looked down at her. 'Who told you?' he asked sharply.

'Why—Giles, but I knew before about— about it, but not who else was involved—at least I did not remember the name.'

The hurt on his face was more than she could bear.

'Oh Jonathan, I'm sorry—I should not have said anything. I should not have caused you to remember her, forgive me,' she said softly.

'I'll see about your trunks, Vinny,' Giles said gruffly, and disappeared swiftly into the crowd.

Jonathan and Lavinia found themselves alone. They faced each other amidst the scurrying travellers, but alone in the crowd.

'It's not remembering which hurts, Vinny, but that you should know.'

'Why—why should it matter my knowing?'

He took her hands in his. 'I'm not proud of what happened, Vinny, in fact I've always regretted it.'

She smiled, anxious to excuse him. 'You were young and impetuous—like Giles is now. He meant no harm in telling me—he was angry on your behalf. You see, Lord Selwyn was with us.'

'With you?' Jonathan himself was angry now. 'He didn't—I mean . . .' Jonathan commanded his emotions quickly and managed to say calmly, but not before she had seen how her meeting Lord Selwyn distressed him, 'What did you think of him?'

She answered truthfully. 'Handsome and charming.'

Jonathan's face clouded.

'But hard and,' she continued, 'I would say cruel. The only person he cares for—and I would guess ever will—is Francis, Viscount Selwyn.'

Relief flooded Jonathan's eyes.

'You had me worried for a moment. I thought perhaps you had fallen for his charms.'

She smiled, a little sadly. 'You need never worry about that, Jonathan, about me falling for the wrong man.'

'How do you know . . .?'

'I've got all your trunks and things,' interrupted Giles. 'Shall we go—or we'll never make it to the hotel in all this commotion.'

Lavinia heard Jonathan's exasperated sigh, but there was nothing to do but follow Giles.

Chapter Eight

The surprise which had been apparent on the faces of both Giles
and Jonathan on their first sight of the changed Lavinia was repeated
in the expressions of her grandfather and the Eldons.

Lord Rowan was staying with Lord and Lady Melmoth and so
it was to 'Eldon House' the brothers took her the following day.

There was no ceremony about the greeting she received. As soon
as the carriage stopped before the front door Lord Rowan—limping
slightly Lavinia noticed immediately—closely followed by Lord and
Lady Melmoth, appeared on the steps. Jonathan gave her his hand
as she stepped from the carriage. But then she ran forward into
her grandfather's outstretched arms.

'Lavinia, my dear, dear child. Let me look at you,' he said when
they had embraced and he held her at arm's length. 'My dear
child—no, I am wrong—you are no longer a child but a young
woman.' She saw the unshed tears glint in his eyes. 'So like Mélanie,'
he added very softly, 'in fact, *exactly* like Mélanie now.'

' 'Pon my soul!' Lord Melmoth demanded of his wife. 'Is it the
same girl?'

'It is indeed. Lavinia my dear,' as she greeted her. 'There, didn't
I tell you, Rupert?' she added as the merry family party made their
way into the house.

The evening was a gay affair, Lavinia being the centre of attention
and enjoying every moment. She had waited so long to be back
here amongst the people she loved and to be worthy of their
company—and to find that they were genuinely delighted in her
maturity was all she could hope for—or almost.

Though still a little shy of Jonathan—perhaps merely because she was fearful she would give away her feelings for him—she was now, nevertheless, able to meet his gaze, to converse with him without blushing in embarrassment and even to tease him a little as he and Giles teased her. Only once during that first evening did she feel a little disconcerted, a little of the old unsureness creeping back to prove that she was not wholly changed. The cause of this was once more the impetuous Giles.

The family were, naturally, eager to hear of her life abroad, of the friends she had made—though she was careful for the moment to avoid the topic of the Selwyns—and of all she had learnt. Without thinking, Giles said, 'And what of your drawings, Vinny, have you been committing more of old Jonathan's face to paper?' Then swiftly realising his error he added, 'And all of us, of course. I hope you've done some more of me.'

Lavinia hesitated—lost in confusion for a brief moment, her heart pounding wildly lest Jonathan or any member of the family should question her closely about her sketches, the ones Giles knew about. Recovering, she decided that there could be no harm in the family seeing the drawings and paintings she had done in France, for there she had been careful to do only an equal number of Jonathan as of the rest of the family.

'As a matter of fact, Madame Givelle was very encouraging. She allowed me to use water colour and even oils on several occasions.'

'Have you brought them back with you?' Giles asked eagerly, and when she nodded, he added, 'Do fetch them—please?'

She smiled at her grandfather who nodded. 'Please, Lavinia.'

She rose. Her grandfather had known of her sketching but had never asked to be shown her work until now.

She fetched the folder of her work from her trunk and three oil paintings—one of Jonathan, one of Giles and one of her grandfather.

'I didn't have time to do one in oils of you, Lady Melmoth, or Lord Melmoth, or I would have done. As you can imagine, oils are rather more expensive and there was only a limited amount available.'

She laid the folder and paintings down on a small side table.

'Which do you want to see first?'

'The oil paintings,' said Giles excitedly. 'Stand over there, Vinny, and we'll view from here.'

She took the three paintings to the far side of the room and held up the one of her grandfather first.

'My goodness!' said Lord Rowan.

'Vinny!' cried Giles.

'Good Lord,' exclaimed Lord Melmoth whilst Lady Melmoth clapped her hands and said, 'Lavinia dear, it's wonderful.'

But Lavinia's eyes were on Jonathan's face. His eyes were intent upon the picture, then his gaze met her eyes. He was the only one who had said nothing.

Slowly, he smiled and she knew in a moment that he too liked the painting but was less voluble in his enthusiasm than the rest.

'Then there's this one of Giles.' She held up the portrait of the laughing Giles. She had caught his impish humour to perfection. The family laughed delightedly.

'Oh I say,' Giles laughed the loudest of all. 'Vinny, please may I have it?'

'Of course. If you like.'

Shyly now, she picked up the one of Jonathan and turned it towards them. She knew herself that she had put her heart and soul into this painting of Jonathan and she held her breath for fear anyone would guess.

There was a small silence before Lord Rowan said, 'That's really excellent, my child. They are all good, but that one . . .'

Oh dear, she thought, he'll give the game away. She dare not look at Jonathan, but put the painting down and turned quickly to the folder of her sketches.

'I've some here of Lord Melmoth and you too. Lady Melmoth.'

These were passed round being smaller than the paintings and also they did not need the distance at which the oils needed to be viewed.

'Lavinia, you indeed have a great talent, my dear. I had no idea. I do wish you had shown me your work earlier,' Lord Rowan said with some regret. 'Perhaps Madame Givelle's school was not the right one in view of this, perhaps I should have sent you to a school of art.'

'Oh no, Grandfather,' Lavinia cried. 'No one could have been kinder or have done more for me than Madame Givelle.'

'I say, look at this one of me, Evelina,' Lord Melmoth chuckled delightedly. 'It's really quite exciting to have one's portrait done. Rowan, you must supply the girl with oils—she must do us some more oil paintings. These sketches are good, but those paintings, especially that one of Jonathan, are superb. I say—hold it up again, Jonathan. Let's all have another look.'

Lavinia gasped and turned in surprise to see that Jonathan had moved, unnoticed whilst the others were looking at the sketches to pick up the portrait of himself and was standing looking down at it. Reluctantly almost, he held it turned away from himself towards the others, and as he did so his eyes met Lavinia's. She saw the question in his eyes—a question she could not and would not answer. Why was the painting of him so much better than the others?

'I still think the one of me is the best,' Giles remarked and picked it up. Lavinia felt a flash of warmth towards him for his thought—she guessed Giles, knowing her secret, was trying to divert the attention away from the portrait of Jonathan. He was successful in his endeavour, but a little time later Jonathan catching her for a moment apart from the rest said in his soft tones.

'Vinny, may I too ask for my portrait?'

She looked up at him, startled for a moment.

'If you wish, b-but it isn't as g-good as they make out.'

He smiled. 'Dear Vinny,' his voice was no more than a whisper. 'You haven't changed so much, after all.'

He turned on his heel abruptly and left the room, pausing only to pick up the portrait of himself which he tucked possessively under his arm.

Lavinia watched him go. Much as she loved him, she would never understand him, she thought.

Later, Giles apologised for his thoughtless slip regarding her drawings, which could have caused her more embarrassment than it had done.

'Vinny—I'm sorry. When will I learn to guard my foolish tongue?'

'No harm done, Giles.'

'I know—but it could have embarrassed you considerably. I'm truly sorry and yet, I'm glad it gave us a chance to see your work. I'm really delighted with this,' he indicated the portrait of himself.

'Lavinia,' she turned to see Lady Melmoth beckoning her to sit beside her on the chaise-longue. 'We must discuss some of the details, my dear, for your coming out. As you know your grandfather has asked me to make all the necessary arrangements, which,' she glanced smilingly at Lord Rowan, 'he knows will give me interminable pleasure.'

Lord Rowan and her husband joined in laughter.

'Firstly, we must arrange a grand ball at your grandfather's house.'

'At "Avonridge"?' Lavinia asked.

'Oh no, here in town. This is to celebrate your homecoming. You must let me know if there is anyone whom you met whilst in France you would like me to invite.'

Lady Melmoth continued whilst Lavinia found Giles watching her, his face unusually serious. No doubt he was thinking of her particular friend, Phillippa Selwyn, and wondering whether Lavinia would invite her and her brother to the ball.

Jonathan returned at that moment and came to stand beside the sofa to listen to his mother recounting all that she had planned for Lavinia. He looked down at Lavinia, amusement in his brown eyes.

'It would seem, Vinny, that you will be occupied for upwards of a year, but don't forget the most important event some time in September.'

She looked at him questioningly.

'You are committed—whether you like it or not—to launch your namesake, the "Lavinia".'

'Oh!' Lavinia clasped her hands delightedly. 'But that is the best yet. Oh, I don't mean to be ungrateful, Lady Melmoth, but that is—well—something special, is it not?'

Lady Melmoth laughed and glanced with affection at her son and Lavinia.

'Of course it is "special" to all of us and since it is named after you, naturally you must launch it.'

'Are things going well, now?' Lavinia turned back to Jonathan, who seated himself beside her. 'No more trouble?'

'Not at present,' he sighed and the smile left his face to be replaced by a worried frown. 'But things are very unsettled.'

Lavinia saw him glance at Lord Rowan in unspoken question.

'You may as well tell her, my boy. She must know sooner or later.'

Lavinia looked from Lord Rowan back to Jonathan. He in turn regarded her face intently for a few moments—she had the fleeting impression he was absorbing every detail of her face as if to imprint it indelibly on his memory.

There was silence in the room as they all waited for Jonathan to speak. He sighed softly so that no one but Lavinia could have heard it. He seemed to pause to recollect his thoughts, as if something had caused him to forget what he had been about to say.

'We couldn't tell you everything in letters, Lavinia, it would not have been prudent. Hostilities between the Keldon Line and Thorwald, Myron and Company have grown considerably. Although they have not—to date—attempted further sabotage of the steamship, our informants tell us that they are nevertheless scheming to bring about our downfall.'

'But what can they do?'

'As you know, the steamship is virtually untried as yet, and whilst we,' he included everyone present, 'have faith in its potential there are many who are sceptical. At the same time there are those who fear its success—as do Thorwald and Myron for if it succeeds, the days of the clipper ships are numbered and for those companies who have not had the foresight to plan to turn over—eventually—to steam, it could spell ruin.'

'I see. And Thorwald and Myron do not intend to invest in a steamship.'

'No—they have not the capital. You see, because it is yet unproved, it is a financial gamble. Let's face it—if we fail, we could be ruined.'

'Come, my boy. Severely hit maybe,' said Lord Rowan, 'but we have not sunk our "all" into this venture, although we do have great hopes of its success.'

'So Thorwald and Myron,' said Lavinia thoughtfully, 'must see to it that our steamship fails to ensure their own survival.'

'Exactly.'

'I see.'

There was a moment's pause before she added quietly. 'I suppose my father and brother are still in partnership with them.'

Jonathan hesitated as if unwilling to hurt her. 'Yes, I fear so.'

She looked down at her hands ashamed of her connection with such rivals who would stop at nothing to bring ruin upon the man she loved. Then, remembering, she looked up to meet Lord Rowan's eyes. He too, after all, was as closely related to them as she was herself.

'We are unfortunate in our connections, are we not, Grandfather?'

He nodded. 'It is a blessing we have each other now, my dear.'

Jonathan's hand covered hers briefly in a swift gesture of comfort, then he rose and left her abruptly, but not before his action had brought tears of gratitude and love to Lavinia's eyes.

During the months that followed her return however, Lavinia had little time to worry unduly about the growing hostilities between the rival companies, for her life was a whirl of social gaiety and the most enjoyable was to be the ball given for her by her grandfather.

It was to be held at Lord Rowan's town house, which had been closed down for a number of years since his virtual retirement to 'Avonridge'. But he re-opened the house now for Lavinia's benefit, for not only must she entertain her guests somewhere in town, but during the Season she could not impose upon the Eldons' hospitality too long. Lord Rowan, much to his surprise, found that city life was not so wearisome as it had previously become now that he had Lavinia with him. Now she was home with him again, he had no great desire to return to Warwickshire alone, but decided to remain in London with her. The Eldon brothers—particularly Giles—were happy to act as Lavinia's escorts to the various functions to which she found herself invited.

'I don't doubt, Jonathan,' Giles would say teasingly to him in Lavinia's presence, 'that you and I will have to fight off all the many suitors for Lavinia's hand.' And he would assume a mournful expression.

'Ah, but you must not fight them *all* off, Giles,' she would respond playfully, 'only the less desirable ones.'

To which Giles would reply, clutching his heart dramatically. 'Ah, why dost thou wound me so, fair maiden, dost thou not know I pine daily for thy favours?'

Whereupon Lavinia would dissolve into unladylike giggles, whilst Jonathan would smile his curious half-smile and finger the scar on his cheek thoughtfully. Who would have thought that the woe-begone, shy child Lavinia had been could be transformed into a confident, self-possessed young woman, well able to match Giles' teasing.

The invitation, which Lavinia wished to extend to Phillippa Selwyn to attend the ball, caused her some concern and she felt obliged to discuss the matter with Jonathan, for she did not wish to cause the Eldons any embarrassment as they, naturally, were her principal guests—but she felt that if Jonathan himself were agreeable then the other members of his family would follow suit.

She did not relish the prospect of raising the subject with him again, for the last time it had been mentioned, the day she had returned from France, he had obviously been disturbed to learn she knew of the incident between Viscount Selwyn and himself.

Unfortunately, Jonathan was at this time a difficult person with whom to hold a conversation, for when he was not actually absent for several days at a time, he always seemed anxious to be off again—his preoccupation with the steamship increasing each day.

One Sunday afternoon, Lavinia decided to take the landau to 'Eldon House', thinking that Jonathan could not possibly be engaged in business upon the Sabbath. She knew too that she did not need to be ceremonious about her visits there, as she was treated as one of the family. The August day was warm and she took a great deal of trouble over her appearance. Her dress was emerald green silk with matching frills being the new style—less crinoline, but draped at the back to form a bustle and train. The bodice was tight-fitting with white lace at her throat. Her hat, matching green, had a white feather. Her parasol too was emerald.

The drive to 'Eldon House' was pleasant, but she enjoyed it with only half her attention for her mind was preoccupied with the speech she proposed to deliver to Jonathan. She alighted from the vehicle and entered the house, the butler opening the door immediately the landau drew up. The butler announced her and she went into the drawing-room to greet Lady Melmoth.

'My dear Lavinia, what a pleasant surprise.'

'Good afternoon, Lady Melmoth. I really came to see Jonathan—is he at home?'

'Why yes. I believe he is in the little room he calls his study. You know where it is?'

'Yes.'

'Then ran along and find him, dear.' Lady Melmoth smiled and watched the girl go, thoughtfully. Now why, she pondered, should Lavinia seem rather agitated? Lady Melmoth shrugged and picked up her book again.

Lavinia made her way through the numerous corridors to the back of the house where she knew Jonathan's study to be. She knocked on the door and hearing his soft tones call 'come in' she entered. He was sitting at a desk, but not working. He was leaning back in his chair his elbows resting on each arm of the chair, his finger-tips together. He was staring up at the portrait of himself which Lavinia had painted and which now hung above the fireplace directly opposite his desk.

'What is it?' he said absently without turning, obviously thinking it was one of the servants.

'I w-wanted to talk to you, Jonathan,' Lavinia said hesitantly.

She saw him jump and when he leapt up and turned to look at her, the startled expression on his face surprised her.

'Vinny! I was just thinking about you—I mean—' he ran his

hand through his hair. She had never seen him so disconcerted before, but the next moment he was in command of himself again and later she wondered if she had misunderstood his words. Could he have been so lost in thought—as he obviously had been—on account of her and the portrait which seemed to command his attention?

'Come and sit down. What brings you to "Eldon House"? I would have thought you would have been out driving with an admirer on such a beautiful afternoon.'

She laughed gaily as she sat down. 'Perhaps I would be, if I *had* an admirer.'

He stood beside her chair and looked down at her for a moment before turning away and going to stand beside the window. He leant against the frame and turned back to face her, so that his face was in shadow whilst the light was full on her.

'Jonathan—I want to ask you something. It's rather— difficult—rather personal—so forgive me if . . .' she paused, took a deep breath and began again. 'You will be coming to the ball, won't you?'

'Why, of course. I wouldn't miss that for the world,' he said softly.

'Well—you know of my friendship with Phillippa Selwyn. Would it cause you or your family embarrassment if I sent her an invitation?—I would not ask her brother, of course, but I'm sure she would feel hurt if she were not invited. But on the other hand,' Lavinia rushed on, rather disconcerted by Jonathan's silence as he stood, quite still, in the semi-shadow. 'If it would prevent you or any of your family from attending, or cause you any—any embarrassment, then I won't invite her.'

The room was still, the only sound being the steady ticking of the mahogany grandfather clock in the corner, as Lavinia waited anxiously for Jonathan's reply. Had she angered or offended him?

'Is it so important to you that I—that we—should attend in preference to Lady Phillippa?' Jonathan's deep tones asked.

'But of *course*,' she said her brown eyes widening in surprise. 'How can you ask such a thing? You know how much you—all your family mean to me,' she blushed and looked down at her lap, her fingers plucking nervously at her lace gloves. Jonathan turned away quickly and looked out of the window. There was an even longer pause. At last he said, 'Send an invitation to your friend—Lord Francis too, if you wish—all that happened a long time ago and is best forgotten by all concerned.'

Lavinia fancied she detected a note of bitterness creep into his tone.

'No—I shall not ask Lord Francis for I don't like him much anyway, but I shall ask Phillippa, if you're really sure . . .'

Jonathan turned from the window and came to stand before her as she rose now to leave. He took her hands in his.

'It was sweet of you to be so concerned on my behalf, my dear. But I wish you had known nothing of the incident.'

She smiled gently at him, loving him the more for admitting his shame. The face of Lady Anthea floated before her. Tears welled in Lavinia's eyes as she imagined the suffering Lady Anthea had caused Jonathan.

'My only sorrow is how you were hurt by it all.' She bent her head briefly and laid her cheek against his hand for an instant. Then, astonished and chagrined by her own daring and revealing show of emotion, she pulled herself free and ran from the room without looking back.

Lavinia did not see any of the Eldon family again before the ball and the lapse of time allowed her to hope that Jonathan would have forgotten her rash, display of affection towards him.

Her excitement grew as the evening approached. Her delight in her new ballgown knew no bounds. It was white silk, the low neckline trimmed with lace which also edged the folds of the train. The over-skirt, decorated with pink roses, was looped beneath which the material was pleated. She wore long gloves, pink to match the roses, and her black hair, with small curls framing her forehead, was dressed in a profusion of ringlets cascading to her shoulders.

Lavinia had, as she had told Jonathan, invited Phillippa only and not Lord Francis. She was unconcerned whether her action in so doing caused a stir in various social circles. Jonathan's feelings were far more important to her than the whispers behind fluttering fans and gloved hands.

Lavinia and her grandfather stood at the foot of the six steps which led down from the double doors into the ballroom and as each guest was announced they greeted them as they came down the stairs into the ballroom. Many of the guests were entirely unknown to Lavinia herself but were families whom her grandfather knew and whom he thought it polite to invite. Several of the younger guests were the friends and acquaintances Lavinia had made since her return from France, when her life had become a social whirl. Many of the young men were anxious to claim a dance with her and Lavinia soon found her programme filling up rapidly. She watched the door anxiously for the arrival of the Eldons, for she did not want her card to be completely filled before Jonathan, and of course Giles too, had at least had had an opportunity of claiming a dance with her.

'You look very charming in that gown, my dear,' remarked her grandfather, when there was a pause between the arrival of guests. She smiled up at him, her brown eyes dancing.

'Then it is all thanks to you, dear Grandfather. I can never thank you enough for having changed my life from what it was to all this.'

He patted her hand. 'All the thanks I need are to see you happy—you are happy?'

'Yes, yes I am,' she squeezed his arm and glanced up at the doors as the Eldons were announced. 'Even more so now,' she murmured, and though she had not intended her grandfather should hear, she realised he had done so for he gave her hand an answering squeeze in understanding, although she knew he would not know to which of the two brothers standing side by side at the top of the stairs she had given her heart.

'Vinny, you look absolutely beautiful,' Giles came bounding down the stairs followed more sedately by Lord and Lady Melmoth and Jonathan.

'Good evening, sir. Let me have your card, Vinny, before all the dances are taken. Ah, only just in time I see. Now, that one and that one ...'

'Now Giles, leave some for me,' and adroitly Jonathan flicked her card from Giles' fingers and casually pencilled his own name beside the three remaining dances on her card. He returned her programme to her with a slight bow.

'Oh well, I got two,' Giles grinned and winked in conspiracy at her.

Later, examining her card to see whom her various partners were, Lavinia saw that two of the dances with Jonathan were the waltz. How fortunate that she had learnt to waltz at school in France.

Lavinia danced several dances with young men anxious, she knew, to charm her, whilst in themselves she found no fault, she could have no interest in them. Then as the orchestra drifted into the three/four time she knew it was time for Jonathan's first dance. Patiently, she waited until he should claim her, willing herself not to search the ballroom for her.

'Vinny, may I claim this dance?' said a soft voice at her elbow and there he was. She rose and he slipped his arm about her waist. They slid gracefully and easily into the steps as if they belonged together. His chin was no more than an inch from her forehead and his nearness to her made her heart pound.

'I haven't seen you dancing before, Jonathan,' she looked up at him.

He was smiling down at her with that curious half-smile.

'I have been waiting until now—until my dance with you.'

She lowered her eyes as a quick thrill of delight ran through her to think that he had been uninterested in dancing until his dance with her.

They danced on in silence.

All too quickly the music ended and her first dance with Jonathan was over. He raised her hand to his lips.

'Until the next waltz, Vinny.' And he left her quickly and moved through the throng of guests. She watched him go, her eyes following him until her next partner claimed her attention.

A little later, Lavinia found herself partnered by Giles in a quadrille.

'You look absolutely lovely, Vinny. You know, I still can't get over the change in you. Why, you're the prettiest girl here.'

Lavinia laughed at his flattery, but nevertheless she enjoyed hearing his words.

Just as their dance was coming to an end, there was a stir amongst the guests and whispers. Simultaneously, Lavinia and Giles turned towards the door and saw the reason for the disturbance.

At the top of the stairs surveying the gathering was Lady Anthea Thorwald, resplendent in a gown of midnight blue, cut very low to reveal her lovely white shoulders and neck. And at her side, of all people, was Lord Francis, Viscount Selwyn.

Lavinia gasped and turned to Giles.

'Giles—what are they doing here?'

'Eh—what?' As he turned she saw his face was serious—gone in an instant was all his gaiety.

'Giles, I didn't send either of them an invitation. Why—how do they come to be here?'

His face hardened. 'They mean to cause you—and all of us I shouldn't wonder—a great deal of embarrassment.'

The other guests, over their initial surprise, resumed their dancing, but Giles and Lavinia moved to the side.

Lady Anthea descended the stairs on Lord Francis' arm, smiling smugly to herself, obviously well-satisfied with the stir their entrance had caused.

'Oh dear,' Lavinia sighed, 'Jonathan will think I invited Lord Selwyn, but I told him I would not do so.'

'They're talking to your grandfather. What impertinence they've got! They know Lord Rowan is too much of a gentleman to ask them to leave, or do anything other than say they're welcome.'

At that moment, Lavinia found herself whisked away by her next partner. She knew she was ungracious towards the young man for throughout the dance she was preoccupied with her thoughts.

The arrival of Lord Selwyn and Lady Anthea had undoubtedly spoilt the evening for her. The next dance was her second waltz with Jonathan and whilst she would not have sought him out, her partner happened to leave her at the end of the dance close to where Jonathan and Giles were talking in low voices. Lavinia tried to turn away, but Jonathan raised his voice.

'Don't ran away, Vinny, is it not our waltz next?'

She felt herself blushing faintly, but she moved forward to join them. Her eyes sought Jonathan's face—was he distressed by the arrival of Lady Anthea? Did he wonder whether she, Lavinia, had after all invited Lord Selwyn and so prompted the arrival not only of him but also of Lady Anthea too?

His expression told her nothing.

'Jonathan, I ...' she began, but at that moment she heard a soft voice and a swish of a gown behind her and she caught the scent of exquisite perfume. Lavinia saw Jonathan's eyes leave hers and seek those of Lady Anthea.

'Jonathan—how wonderful!'

'Lady Anthea,' Jonathan said politely, but again showing nothing of what he was actually thinking. 'This is somewhat a surprise,' he continued mildly.

'But not unpleasant,' Lady Anthea smiled up at him, her eyes flirting with him.

Lord Selwyn strolled up.

'Ah, the radiant and beautiful Miss Kelvin,' Lord Francis kissed her hand. 'May I have the honour of this next dance—the waltz, I believe?'

'I'm sorry, but ...' she hesitated and cast a pleading glance at Jonathan.

'Miss Kelvin is engaged for the next dance with me.'

'Ah, how de do, Eldon, didn't see you there. Well, I trust? Ha-ha.' And he laughed again.

Jonathan nodded shortly, his eyes unreadable depths.

'Let the children have their dance,' purred Lady Anthea. 'Besides, I want to waltz with you, Jonathan, it's so long since ...' she seemed about to say more but altered her line of conversation. 'After all,' she laughed, 'they are more of an age, don't you think?'

Lord Selwyn joined her in laughter, but neither Jonathan nor Lavinia, nor Giles, who had heard the entire exchange of conversation, found her remark amusing. Indeed, Lavinia thought that Jonathan looked angry. The scar on his cheek seemed to stand out vividly.

'Come then, Miss Kelvin,' Lord Selwyn held out his hand to her as the orchestra began to play.

'Jonathan, I . . .' she hesitated again.

'The child seems incapable of completing a sentence,' remarked Lady Anthea.

Lavinia turned away quickly and found herself in Lord Selwyn's arms being led into the steps of the waltz. She did not look back but kept her eyes fastened on Lord Selwyn's silk waistcoat, so that she would not see Jonathan waltzing with Lady Anthea.

Lavinia remembered little more of the evening for she saw no more of Jonathan. He did not appear to claim his third dance with her. For the remainder of the evening she danced automatically, a fixed smile on her face which she prayed was convincing for the sake of her grandfather. But much later, in the privacy of her room, she was able to give way to the disappointment and she cried herself to sleep over the lost waltz with Jonathan, quite sure that this time her heart was completely broken.

Chapter Nine

The social whirl continued for Lavinia, but she was not as happy now as she had been on her return from France. No doubt, though she had tried not to do so, she had, deep down, nurtured the hope that with her 'transformation' Jonathan would fall in love with her. But it was obvious now, she thought, that he had not done so and that in all probability he was still in love with Lady Anthea. Though why someone with Jonathan's intelligence could not see Lady Anthea for the cruel, shallow woman she was, Lavinia could not understand. Though Cupid is reputedly blind, she thought, and it must be so.

From the night of the ball, Lavinia saw very little of Jonathan, but she began to see a good deal more of one person who she would rather not. have seen—Lord Francis Selwyn. At first she thought that it was merely a coincidence that he should be present at nearly every social event to which she was invited, but as the weeks went by, the number of occasions on which she found herself, through no fault of her own, in his company, it became apparent that these occasions were too frequent to be coincidental. Whenever Giles was her escort, her escape from Lord Selwyn's advances was easy, for he was somewhat unwilling to approach her when she was accompanied by Giles Eldon, who glowered at Francis when they met or deliberately led Lavinia in the opposite direction.

Of course, Lavinia was always properly chaperoned at all the public functions she attended by a married woman, Mrs Jay, whom her grandfather had appointed for that purpose. But Mrs Jay was not always able—or inclined—to fend off the unwelcome attentions which young men paid to Lavinia. Fortunately, for the sake of her reputation, Lavinia was well able to take care of herself. Her kind heart prevented her from telling her grandfather of Mrs Jay's shortcomings as a chaperon, so she continued to try to avoid Lord Selwyn as best she could without being deliberately uncivil to him for the sake of her friendship with Phillippa. In actual fact, she saw less of Phillippa than she had anticipated and had wondered why until, meeting her friend at a ball some weeks after the one given by her grandfather and at which Phillippa had promised to meet Lavinia more frequently, she learnt the reason from Phillippa herself.

'Oh Lavinia, you shall be the first to congratulate me. I am engaged to be married!'

'My dear Phillippa, how happy I am for you,' Lavinia smiled, kissing her friend's cheek.

'Look—there he is, over there, talking to Francis. Don't you think he is the handsomest man you've ever seen?'

Phillippa's fiancé was indeed handsome with a moustache and side-whiskers, but when Phillippa introduced him to her, Lavinia found herself looking into a pair of eyes so cold that she felt a shudder down her spine. There was no humour in this man's personality and the gay Phillippa would find, Lavinia was sure, that her husband-to-be would try to curb her natural high spirits.

'My dear Miss Kelvin, may I have the honour of the next dance?' Lord Francis interrupted his sister's chatter.

Lavinia was forced to acquiesce. They danced in silence but Lord Selwyn's eyes never left her face, and on his thin lips was a small smile as if he were enjoying some private joke. During the evening he claimed a total of four dances with her which Lavinia found herself unable to refuse. She knew it could place her in an awkward situation for social convention was such that if a girl danced with a particular young man three or four times in one evening, it was expected that before long their engagement would be announced.

Worriedly, Lavinia wondered whether Lord Francis was deliberately trying to provoke such a rumour so that Lavinia's friendship with the Eldon family, and with Jonathan in particular, would be put under some strain. Then again, she mused, as her maid brushed her hair for her late that night before retiring, Lord Francis could be trying to ingratiate himself with her in order to find out about the steamship, for perhaps his renewed friendship with Lady Anthea could mean that he too was engaged with the rival company.

But this thought was dispelled a few days later by Giles—though she told him nothing of her thoughts. They were out driving in the landau one sunny afternoon—Lavinia pretty in a summer dress of white muslin over a pale blue taffeta underdress, flounced at the hem. Her small flower-trimmed hat was perched on the front of her hair which was dressed in a smooth chignon in the nape of her neck.

'I can see every other fellow casting envious glances at me,' Giles grinned, 'driving out with the prettiest girl in London.'

Lavinia laughed. 'Where are we going?'

'Wherever you say—your wish is my command.'

'May—may we go and see the steamship?'

Giles looked at her sharply. 'Of course, if you wish. Jonathan will be there.'

'He—he won't mind, will he?'

A worried frown crossed Giles' face. 'No—I don't suppose so, but . . .'

'But what, Giles?'

Giles sighed and seemed embarrassed. 'He's been so odd lately. Bad-tempered, almost—and that's not like him. I know he's a bit of an old sobersides but he's not usually ill-tempered.'

'How long has he been like it? I have not seen him since the ball.'

Giles looked at her again thoughtfully as if her remark had reminded him of something.

'He's been moody since then, I suppose. He spends most of his time either working at the office, or down at Blackwall with the steamship, or shut up in his study at home.'

Lavinia had a mental picture of Jonathan sitting at his desk alone in his study as she had once found him.

'Of course,' Giles was saying slowly, 'it might be something to do with what happened at the ball.'

Lavinia's heart was heavy.

'Lady Anthea, you mean? Do you think he—he still cares for her?'

'Surely not!' Giles exclaimed. 'Why she's creating a bad reputation for herself just lately, you know.'

'No—I didn't know. How do you mean?'

'Well, she appeared at the ball with Lord Selwyn, didn't she?'

'Yes.'

'Since then she's been seen at various events in the company of Viscount Porley, Lord Goreman, Lord Selwyn again,' he ticked off the occasions on his fingers, 'and—believe it or not—with Lord Myron.'

'Good gracious!'

'And on none of those occasions was her husband present. I believe there have been others, too, from what I hear, but those are the only ones I know.'

'I see,' Lavinia said, and thought that Lord Selwyn would probably not be engaged with Lord Thorwald in business but would merely be one of Lady Anthea's many escorts.

'Do you think,' she asked in a small voice, 'that Jonathan has heard this too and is hurt by it?'

'Oh Vinny,' Giles took her hand in his and squeezed it, trying to comfort her for he knew how she must feel, loving Jonathan as he believed she still did. 'I wish I knew but I dare not ask him.' He grinned ruefully. 'For all my brashness, I'm a little afraid of my big brother.'

Lavinia smiled.

The steamship had altered almost beyond recognition since Lavinia had seen it. Where previously there had been a mere skeleton, now there was a ship nearing completion, her sleek lines curving gracefully. Eventually, Giles told Lavinia, the ship would have a funnel to proclaim with pride the fact that she was one of the still rather rare steamships, but her masts would show that she did not spurn the heritage of sail. She was merely a vessel trying to move forward into the future and yet at the same time acknowledging the debt she owed to the past.

Giles brought the landau to a halt and they walked the short distance to stand near the *Lavinia*.

'Isn't it big, Giles? I had no idea it was such a size.' Lavinia craned her neck to look up at the ship which towered above them. They stood some moments looking up at the ship before Lavinia said, 'Isn't she beautiful?'

'Just like her namesake,' a soft voice said behind them and they turned to see Jonathan.

Lavinia smiled at his compliment but she was shocked to see the sadness in his eyes. He had reverted from the gay partner he had been at the ball to his previous reserved and solemn manner. His face was a little thinner and the scar ugly. She had never seen him look so unhappy.

An overwhelming desire to comfort him made her forget her shyness of him and she moved to his side and put her hand through his arm. His eyes never left her face and she had the impression that he was trying to read in her eyes the answer to some question. She smiled gently at him, trying to tease him out of his present mood.

'I've not seen you these past weeks. Have you deserted me entirely?'

Not even the ghost of his half-smile could be coaxed to his lips.

'I thought you had plenty of eligible company and that you would not need me.' His deep voice was low.

She sighed and her mock show of petulance at his neglect of her held more truth than she hoped he would guess.

'I see I am deserted in favour of a ship,' she moaned, but her eyes twinkled merrily at him.

'But she is named after you,' he said, and gradually the gentle smile appeared—tentatively, as if unused for some time.

'Huh, first time I've seen him smile in weeks,' Giles grunted. 'Seems you can thaw an iceberg, Vinny.'

'It seems she's thawed a good many icebergs from what I hear.'

'What have you been hearing, Jonathan?'

'Oh, that you have all the eligible bachelors at your feet.'

She laughed. 'Nonsense.'

'There's only one she . . .' Giles began and stopped, appalled at his stupidity. He turned and hurried away leaving Lavinia alone with Jonathan, her heart pounding for fear he should question her. So close to him, she doubted her ability to hide her feelings for him. But when she dared to glance at him, his eyes were not on her but were fixed straight ahead on his steamship. He began to speak about the arrangements for the launching, ignoring Giles' remark entirely.

Lavinia noticed, however, that the smile had disappeared from his face completely and his eyes took on a haunted, defeated expression. Whether or not this was caused by what he chose to read into Giles' remark, Lavinia could not guess. Instead, she tried to concentrate on what Jonathan was saying and take an interest in the steamship.

'Have there been any more attempts at sabotage, Jonathan?'

'No—thank goodness, though there have been rumours that another attempt might be made. The previous time caused a lot of excitement and speculation in the city. Of course, we're trying to take greater security precautions now, but I must admit that I am surprised our rivals have tried nothing more.'

Perhaps, thought Lavinia, Lady Anthea has been instrumental in what seemed to be a withdrawal of opposition. Perhaps, with her recent renewal of contact with Jonathan, Lady Anthea found she really did still have some affection for him and had therefore persuaded her husband to cease hostilities.

At that moment Giles rejoined them.

'It's time I took you home, Vinny,' he said in a subdued voice and she saw the silent apology written in his eyes. She smiled at him and he, seeing this, looked somewhat relieved.

'When is the launching to take place, Jonathan?' Lavinia asked as they moved towards the landau.

'About three weeks from now.'

'How lovely—I'm looking forward to it enormously. Grandfather is inviting you all to dine with us afterwards—you will come, won't you?'

'Of course.'

As the landau moved away Lavinia turned to wave to Jonathan as he stood, a lonely figure, watching them out of sight.

Although Lavinia's excitement at the forthcoming launching of the steamship grew, it seemed as if the Fates were conspiring to spoil every event upon which she pinned special hopes regarding Jonathan.

First, there had been the time, when on her departure for France, she had been overjoyed to think that Jonathan had come to Dover to say goodbye to her, and Giles had dashed that pleasure by telling her that Jonathan was there on business anyway. The second occasion had been the ball and the dances which Lady Anthea had stolen from her and to add to this was the fact that she had seen Jonathan only once since, and then his mood had seemed so strange.

Now, when she had anticipated the launching of the *Lavinia* with such delight, again a disappointment awaited her.

The day of the launching arrived. Lavinia was in a fever of excitement. She had looked forward to this day for so long. She took a long time to dress and then went to find her grandfather in the long drawing-room.

'Do I look all right, Grandfather?' She pirouetted gracefully before him.

Her dress was royal blue, the skirt with the draped bustle effect which was now rapidly becoming popular. Her matching hat was trimmed with a paler blue ribbon and was perched on the front of her head. She again wore her hair in a smooth chignon at the back of her head. Her gloves and parasol were a pale blue to match the ribbon trimming on her hat. The short, tight-fitting coat was royal blue.

'Perfect, my dear.'

'I thought the plainer material and less frills and feathers more befitting the occasion.'

'But you'll wear that pretty evening gown tonight—the new lemon one?'

She laughed. 'The one that's a profusion of frills and roses—yes, if you like it.'

'I think it suits your colouring, my dear,' he smiled. 'But any colour seems to suit you—you look enchanting whatever you wear. Come, it is time we went to 'Eldon House' and collected the others. We're all travelling in my carriage—it's big enough to hold the six of us.'

The Eldons were waiting for them and they left immediately.

As the carriage sped towards Blackwall, Giles burst out.

'Have you heard the news, Lord Rowan, Jonathan has only just told us?'

'Depends what it is, my boy,' Lord Rowan remarked. 'Can't say I can think we've heard anything of import recently, have we, Lavinia, my dear?'

'I don't think so, Grandfather.' She looked towards Jonathan anxiously. 'Is it something to do with the ship?'

'No,' he said slowly. 'Not directly, though I suppose it could ultimately affect the present situation.'

'What is it?' Lavinia asked, her wide eyes never leaving his face.

'Lord Thorwald has died.'

'What?' exclaimed her grandfather, but Lavinia merely gasped and turned pale. As if about to speak the very thought she herself had, Giles burst out, 'Affect the situation? Jonathan, you don't mean you'd—oh no, dash it all!' Then realising the rashness of his words Giles reddened and subsided into silence. Jonathan merely glanced affectionately at his brother and smiled quietly to himself. Everyone in the carriage was uncomfortably aware that Giles' question had been provoked by Jonathan's remark that Lord Thorwald's death could affect the present situation existing between the rival companies. Giles, and possibly everyone else, thought that Jonathan meant that a change in the present circumstances would be brought about because Lady Anthea was now free to marry again and if he were to propose to her and be accepted, the two companies would be somewhat united by their marriage.

'Er—um. Well, now,' Lord Melmoth broke the uneasy silence. 'Can't pretend much regret, though I didn't wish the fellow any personal harm. Mind you,' he added wisely, wagging his forefinger, 'he wasn't the most dangerous of our rivals—you mark my words.'

'Quite so, Rupert,' agreed his wife, and, with her eyes on her eldest son, she added, 'I should not be surprised if his wife were not one of the prime movers against us.'

The subject was closed, but remained in the minds of them all, and for Lavinia the day which had begun so light-heartedly was in one short moment spoilt.

'Good gracious, there's quite a few people here, Rowan,' Lord Melmoth remarked as the carriage drew to a halt near the steamship. 'Didn't realise it had created quite so much interest, did you?'

'I know there's been a lot of talk about it in the city, especially since the sabotage episode.'

'You don't think they'll try anything today, do you?' Giles asked. There was a slight pause.

'I don't think so—I don't think they'd want to risk harming innocent people,' Jonathan said. 'You're not afraid, are you, Lavinia?'

'Only for the ship,' was her reply.

'We'll stick close by you, anyway,' Giles said. 'Mama, you stay close to Father and Lord Rowan. We'll look after Vinny.'

Lavinia, with Jonathan and Giles close beside her, climbed to the platform where the traditional bottle of champagne was held in place until she released it to fall against the ship. In her clear, steady voice she said, 'I name this ship the *Lavinia*. May God bless her and all who sail in her.'

Privately she added 'and God bless the man whose pride she is.' She let the bottle swing towards the ship. It smashed at once, splashing champagne in all directions. A few drops fell on Lavinia's dress. The crowd cheered and the ship began to move, gathering speed until it hit the water. It was a wonderful moment, but an anxious one for in these first few moments the ship had to prove her ability to float. Gradually the water, disturbed by the ship plunging into it, calmed and she lay peacefully below them as if quite ready to begin her maiden voyage without further delay.

Lavinia turned to look at Jonathan, who was standing beside

her. His face was animated with pride and a fire glowed in his usually calm eyes. He turned and met her gaze.

'Isn't she beautiful? Isn't she perfect? Look at that line?'

He looked back to the ship. 'My goodness, we'll show those clippers.'

Lavinia followed his gaze and ran her eyes over the sleek lines of the new ship. There was no doubt about it—the ship was similar in appearance to the clippers but so very different in modus operandi, and she still had to prove herself better than they were. No doubt their rivals were hoping that, as they had failed to prevent the completion of the steamship and the launching, the *Lavinia* would now fail in proving herself better than the clippers.

The Eldons returned with Lavinia and Lord Rowan but went on to 'Eldon House' and returned to dine later in the evening.

Lavinia, as she had promised her grandfather, wore the gown he favoured. Her hair she had dressed in a more elaborate style than the chignon, high on her head but with ringlets and curls. But gone was all the joy with which she had awoken that morning. She sighed as she descended the stairs to join her grandfather and the Eldons in the drawing-room and realised that she must try her best to be cheerful for no one must guess how the thought that Lady Anthea was once more free to marry affected her.

'Vinny, how beautiful you look,' Giles greeted her, his wide grin as beaming as ever, as if he had forgotten all about his previous remark in the carriage, or perhaps, she thought, he had not realised how his insinuation regarding a possible marriage between Jonathan and Lady Anthea could hurt her.

'Indeed you do, my dear, doesn't she, Jonathan?' said Lady Melmoth.

'But she always looks beautiful,' he murmured. The half-smile was there as if he had no other thought in his head beyond paying petty compliments to Lavinia Kelvin. He moved towards her and standing close said softly so that no one else could hear,

'Don't be offended, my dear, but I do like your hair the way it is tonight.'

His fingers touched one of her ringlets gently. 'The style you wore this afternoon was sophisticated, but far too severe for you.'

Despite the ache in her heart, she smiled, amused to think that he had noticed her hair.

'Then,' she said playfully but meaning it, 'I shall never wear it that way again.'

Jonathan gave one of his rare chuckles and offered her his arm as dinner was announced.

The table was a magnificent sight, for, to add to the fine silver and glassware, was the centre piece—an archway of about five feet high and four feet wide of red roses and fern, beneath which stood a small silver vase of white roses. At either end of the table stood two more identical vases of white roses.

'Wilford,' exclaimed Lady Melmoth, 'what beautiful roses and so wonderfully arranged. Whoever have you on your staff who is so artistic?'

Lord Rowan and Lavinia exchanged a smile and as they all took their places, he said mildly,

'Not exactly a member of my staff, Evelina.'

'Oh,' Lady Melmoth said with disappointment, but with a mischievous twinkle in her eyes. 'What a shame. I was hoping to entice whoever it was to join my household.'

'I'm sure,' Lord Rowan replied finding difficulty in hiding his smile, 'that the person concerned would be only too happy to assist you any time.'

A muffled giggle escaped Lavinia.

'Mama,' Giles said, 'I do believe Lord Rowan means Lavinia.'

Lord Rowan and Lavinia laughed together.

'Really?' Lady Melmoth looked a little disconcerted. 'Forgive me, my dear, for being so slow—I should have guessed it was you with your artistic talent. And,' she said smiling again, 'I shall take your grandfather up on his offer on your behalf.'

The meal commenced on this light-hearted note, but it was inevitable that the conversation should return to the topic of the steamship and Lavinia, once more reminded of Lord Thorwald's death and all it could mean, became unusually quiet.

'Perhaps we shall see a little more of you, Jonathan,' his mother remarked, 'now that the steamship has been launched.'

'Indeed,' Lord Rowan said, 'you have taken more than your fair share of the responsibility in this venture—and you have dealt with all the problems admirably.'

'Thank you, sir,' Jonathan said quietly, 'but there is still a great deal to be done before the ship is completed and as we are determined to have her ready to sail about next April, I shall be occupied for some months yet.'

Lavinia, from her position at table between Giles and Jonathan, could not easily see the expression on Jonathan's face, but she could sense that Lord Rowan's brief compliment meant far more to him than all the elaborate flattery he had received during the last few weeks as the building of the steamship progressed.

'You're very quiet, Vinny,' remarked the observant Giles. 'Are you feeling all right?'

'Yes, quite, thank you. A little tired perhaps.'

Everyone turned to look at her.

'You do look a little pale, my dear,' said Lady Melmoth.

'It's the high and giddy life she's been leading catching up with her,' chuckled Giles.

Lavinia saw her grandfather looking concerned, so she smiled brightly at him. She must not allow any one of them to guess the truth for her despondency—the thought that now Lady Anthea was free once more, she, Lavinia, would perhaps lose Jonathan for ever.

'Maybe we should go to 'Avonridge' for a while,' Lord Rowan remarked.

'Why, yes, I would love that. Grandfather,' she said quickly, trying to ignore the feeling of swift disappointment at being parted from Jonathan again.

'Would you all care to come?' Lord Rowan addressed the Eldon family.

'That's very kind of you, Wilford,' Lady Melmoth answered. 'Well, Rupert?'

'Yes, my dear. It would make a welcome change. Rowan. Many thanks. Can't speak for the boys, of course.'

'I should love to come—must get that woe-begone look off Vinny's face, y'know,' smiled Giles. 'And I'm the chap to do it.'

Everyone laughed, but Lavinia was waiting for Jonathan's answer, hardly daring to breathe. She dare not hope that he would want to come with them to 'Avonridge'—no doubt he would wish to stay in town now near Lady Anthea. But she was wrong for Jonathan said, 'I too would very much like to come for a short while. The steamship can take care of itself for a week or two,' he smiled, 'though I mustn't desert her entirely—in fact, I may go on her first trip to China when . . .'

'Oh no,' Lavinia cried before she could stop herself.

Lord Melmoth looked sharply at his son.

'I don't think that would be wise, my boy.'

'There's always Giles to take my place if . . .'

'If you go, I go too,' put in Giles firmly, all trace of his boyishness gone in an instant.

Lavinia heard Jonathan sigh softly. 'There's an end to it then. I can't possibly go.'

'There's something going on here I don't understand,' Lady Melmoth said. 'Will someone please enlighten me?'

Lord Melmoth cleared his throat uncomfortably, but Lord Rowan looked as puzzled as Lady Melmoth and Lavinia were.

'Jonathan has mentioned before that he wanted to go on the steamship's first voyage to China,' Lord Melmoth explained. 'Giles and I are trying to persuade him not to do so.'

'I see. But why exactly?' his wife asked. Lord Melmoth and his sons exchanged glances.

'Her first voyage to China will be a major trial for her. Provided all goes well, she will bring a cargo of tea back—her first. At about the same time—roughly the beginning of next July, we understand that Myron will have a ship—a clipper, of course—due to leave Shanghai and we anticipate that that could be the greatest test for the *Lavinia*. Whichever ship docks in London first will quite probably mean rain for the loser.'

'In short,' added Jonathan, 'the situation will develop into a race. You know the importance now of being the first to dock with a new shipment of tea. Clippers have often raced each other, but this time, with a new steamship involved, the result has more far-reaching effects.'

'Don't you see, Mama,' put in Giles excitedly, 'if the clipper should win—which it won't—Myron's Company will have proved themselves right that the steamship is a failure? But if the steamship docks first, *we* shall be vindicated and prove that the steamship is the ship of the future.'

'And you mean because of the rivalry which will develop there will be actual danger to the *Lavinia* and that's why you do not want Jonathan to go?'

'Precisely, my dear,' her husband replied.

'And, you'll note,' Jonathan put in, smiling gently, 'that I'm being blackmailed. Giles says that if I go, he will go, and naturally I can't endanger him, so . . .'

'Why should you want to endanger yourself?' said Lavinia with some sharpness. 'Do you imagine we care so little for you that . . . that . . .' She stopped, appalled at her own stupidity in betraying her feelings. But Giles, her confidant, came to her rescue by agreeing vehemently with her statement and so minimising the underlying meaning of her words.

'Exactly, the silly goat must think we would happily wave him goodbye not caring whether or not he ever came back,' he snorted. 'You'd think he'd know differently, wouldn't you?'

The other members of the gathering smiled, amused by Giles' outburst and Lavinia hoped fervently that her own impetuous words were forgotten. But some time later, when the gentlemen rejoined the ladies in the drawing-room, Jonathan drew Lavinia to one side and said softly, 'Would you really worry about me, Vinny, if I were to go with the steamship?'

She hesitated, blushing faintly. 'Of course,' she muttered. 'Shouldn't I?' she added defensively.

'But I didn't think you . . .'

'I say, Vinny,' interrupted Giles joining them, 'have you done any more paintings lately? And when are you going to do another of me? I could sit for you, you know.'

Jonathan cursed softly to himself as Lavinia turned her attention to Giles. Could he never converse with Lavinia, Jonathan was thinking, without Giles interrupting? But she, however, was thankful for Giles' intervention. Jonathan subsided into silence and moved away, saying very little during the remainder of the evening.

It was arranged that Lord Rowan and Lavinia should leave for Warwickshire the next day and the Eldons would join them at the week-end giving Lord Rowan time to make the necessary arrangements for entertaining them. By the time the Eldons arrived several days later, Lavinia had composed herself and had with great effort and no little courage, managed to become the cheerful, vivacious girl she was now expected to be all the time. She thrust all thoughts of Jonathan and Lady Anthea aside and concentrated upon assisting her grandfather and enjoying the company of the Eldon family as a whole.

'You look much better now, my dear child,' Lady Melmoth remarked as she kissed Lavinia in greeting.

'It must be 'Avonridge' then, for I love it here,' Lavinia laughed.

Their stay was pleasurable. Lavinia found herself constantly in the company of Giles and Jonathan, though rarely with either of them alone. They became a merry trio—Giles with his usual exuberance, Lavinia with her determined gaiety and even Jonathan was relaxed, and flashes of his youthful impetuosity and frivolity began to reassert themselves. The three went riding together, for Lavinia was now well able to keep pace with their horsemanship. They went for carriage drives and walks through the grounds of 'Avonridge'. But their activities were undertaken at a relaxed, restful pace, entirely different from the hectic whirl of London social life.

'Don't you long for the city?' Giles remarked one sunny afternoon in late September when the three of them were sitting in the garden which had now come to be known as Lavinia's since it was her favourite spot—the garden with the little fountain where Giles had inadvertently stumbled upon Lavinia's secret when he had seen all her drawings of Jonathan.

'No—I don't. Do you?'

'Yes and no. I like it here, don't you, Jonathan?'

Jonathan nodded.

'But,' Giles continued, 'I couldn't stay here for ever.'

'Oh, I could,' sighed Lavinia.

'So could I,' Jonathan murmured. 'But you seemed to be enjoying the city life, Vinny.'

'I did—I suppose. But it's all so— shallow, somehow. I mean, all those balls and dinner parties. What have you got at the end of it?'

'You certainly hide your feelings remarkably well.'

'Oh I did enjoy it, especially at first. And I didn't want to hurt Grandfather. He was doing it all for me—I didn't want to appear ungrateful.'

'You're rather good at hiding your feelings, aren't you, Vinny?' Giles said softly. Lavinia smiled and she saw Jonathan glance at her, a puzzled expression in his eyes.

'It would be unbecoming of a young lady to do otherwise,' she replied flippantly and tried to laugh gaily.

'But I thought you enjoyed the attentions of all those handsome young men?' Giles teased her.

She laughed. 'I'd much rather be here with just the two of you.'

'Really?' Giles beamed at her affectionately, his eyes telling her he understood why, but Jonathan seemed rather surprised.

'Do you mean to say you prefer our dull company to all those handsome, dashing bachelors in town?'

'Dull!' Giles exploded. 'You speak for yourself Lord Eldon. *I'm* not dull, am I, Vinny?'

She laughed. 'Neither of you is dull.'

'But what about James Andover?' Giles teased, mentioning one of the young men who had been an admirer of Lavinia. 'He used to hang upon your every word.'

'And what of Lord Selwyn?' murmured Jonathan, a little too casually.

'I heard before we left town,' Giles said, 'that he'd been seen visiting Lady Anthea.'

Lavinia could not help glancing at Jonathan to see whether Giles' words had any effect. Was it possible, she thought in alarm, that the old rivalry over Lady Thorwald between Lord Francis and Jonathan could be renewed? She was startled to see that Jonathan's eyes were upon her regarding her intently. Swiftly she turned away, and, with more command of the situation than she felt, she tactfully changed the subject.

The Eldons' visit came to an end and when they had gone, Lavinia found 'Avonridge' was not quite the haven she had so strongly claimed it to be—perhaps because Jonathan was no longer there.

However, she still preferred 'Avonridge' to city life for although back in town she would have been nearer Jonathan and more likely to see something of him, nevertheless Lady Anthea, she knew, also remained in the city and Lavinia had no wish to risk encountering Jonathan and Lady Anthea together as she feared they may now often be, in spite of Giles' information that Viscount Selwyn had visited her. Perhaps his call had been merely a courtesy call to express his condolences on the death of her husband, Lavinia thought, for Lord Francis had obviously been on friendly terms with her when her husband had been alive—had he not escorted her to the ball—so it was natural that he should be on hand to offer comfort. But Lavinia's thoughts tortured her. Would Jonathan too want to comfort and console Lady Anthea now, even though he had, she believed, seen little of Lady Thorwald before her husband's death?

The months passed and Christmas—a quiet affair for Lord Rowan and Lavinia—came and went. They saw nothing of the Eldon family during that time for, although they had received an invitation to spend Christmas at 'Eldon House', Lord Rowan was at the time not feeling well and preferred to stay at 'Avonridge'. Lavinia, for her grandfather's sake, hid her disappointment. She heard of the Eldons frequently, though, for Lord Rowan was kept fully informed of the progress of the steamship and Lady Melmoth and Giles wrote to her often.

Winter gave way to spring, and spring to summer, but there was still no word from Jonathan himself.

The *Lavinia* sailed from England in April and at the beginning of July, when news came through that she was laden and ready to leave Shanghai for England, Lord Rowan, his health improved, said, 'Lavinia, I think I should go up to London whilst this business is on. You remember Melmoth telling us about the possibility of a race developing between the *Lavinia* and Myron's clipper?'

'Yes, Grandfather, I do.'

'It looks as if he was right, and that is exactly what is going to happen. In fact, we rather think that Myron and his associates—your father and brother amongst them and, I suppose, Lady Anthea Thorwald—have engineered the whole thing. We believe they *want* a race to develop in an attempt to discredit us.'

'You think you should be on hand in case anything goes wrong.'

'I do, my dear. As you know, Melmoth and his boys do most of the day to day running of the Company, but I feel I should be there to shoulder my share of the responsibility this time.'

'Of course,' Lavinia kissed his temple.

'When do we leave?'

'I don't think you should come, Lavinia. There may be unpleasantness whatever the result of the race. I think you had better stay here.'

'Just you try to keep me away,' she laughed merrily.

There was a moment's pause whilst Lord Rowan appeared to be considering whether to allow her to accompany him.

'Very well, child,' he said gently and the look on his face left her in no doubt that he guessed that there was someone in London whom she wanted to see in spite of herself. In all probability he had eliminated all casual friends and acquaintances down to the two Eldon brothers, but she was sure he could not guess which of them it was.

On their arrival in London they were surprised to find the extent of interest the race was causing amongst people not even connected with the Keldon Line. Other shipping companies divided themselves either on the side of the Keldon Line or in favour of Myron's clipper, according to whether they were forward-thinking persons or old-fashioned sceptics.

From China they received word that the steamship and the clipper had left together.

The race had started.

Day by day the tension mounted. Lord Rowan and Lavinia met with the Eldons frequently and always the major topic of conversation was the race. Jonathan became even more serious, even more wrapped up in the progress of the steamship. His face wore a perpetual frown and the scar was more than ever apparent. Lord Melmoth's agitation showed itself in his restlessness—he would frequently pace about the room. Even Giles had lost much of his natural exuberance. Only Lady Melmoth appeared to retain her serenity, her calm face never showing any disquiet. But to the discerning observer, one feature gave away the fact that she too was anxious—her dark eyes followed the movements of her husband, or searched the sober face of her elder son.

Lord Rowan's presence undoubtedly had a calming influence. The Eldons, though competent themselves, were grateful to have his support. But their concern was minimal in comparison to the anxiety which was about to befall them, when the race had been on for some seven weeks and the ships were about three-quarters of the way home. Poor Giles was inadvertently the cause of the disaster.

The families continued to lead their normal lives as far as possible and Giles was accustomed to frequenting a Gentleman's Club in the city. Although he had attended little of late because of the extra pressure of business, as the tension increased he sought to put all thoughts of the race from his mind, if only for a few hours, and spent an evening at his Club. He dined with friends, who though idly speculative upon the race were not greatly interested in it. Giles played cards with them until midnight and was leaving the Club when a carriage drew up beside him and to his surprise a voice hailed him.

'Eldon—Giles Eldon.'

He turned.

'Eldon—here a minute, if you please.'

Giles could not recognise the voice which was that of a young man. He hesitated, shrugged and decided that no harm could come of it and approached the carriage cautiously.

'I say, Eldon, could you spare a fellow a moment's conversation?'

Giles strained his eyes in the darkness and saw then that it was the face of Roderick Kelvin, Lavinia's brother, peering at him from the carriage window.

'What do you want, Kelvin?' Giles said none too graciously.

'I say—look here—step in here a moment, won't you? I'd like to talk to you.' He opened the door. Again Giles hesitated, but, now intrigued, he gave way and climbed up to sit opposite Roderick in the darkness of the carriage.

'I'll drop you off home, if you like—we'll talk on the way.'

Before Giles could protest, Roderick gave directional instructions to the driver.

'What is all this about, Kelvin?' Giles asked sharply.

'I'll come straight to the point, Eldon. I've never liked what my parents did to Lavinia, you know, and whilst I doubt they'll ever be reconciled with her—not the way they talk about her,' he simpered, 'I don't like being estranged from her. You may not believe me, but I do assure you I'm very fond of her, always have been and I'd like to see her again.'

'Why don't you call on her then?'

'What, at Grandfather's? Out of the question, old fellow, he'd fling me out, I know that.'

'Not if you explained the position to him—especially if you are prepared to leave your parents too.'

'Oh, I ain't prepared to do that—good Lord no—maybe I don't agree with them, but—well—I am provided for, you know.'

Giles merely grunted.

'Look—all I'm asking is for you to tell Lavinia what I've said and if she agrees, I'd like to meet her, say In the gardens tomorrow at three o'clock, just to talk to her. Will you tell her?'

Giles thought for a moment. 'I don't know,' he murmured doubtfully, unable to trust Roderick.

'Oh do, please do, at least tell her—let her decide. If she doesn't want to . . .' he shrugged and sighed expressively, 'then at least I'll have done my part towards reconciliation.'

'All right,' agreed Giles at length though still somewhat reluctantly. 'I'll tell her at least—but I shan't advise her in *any* way what to do—it will be her decision.'

The next morning, Giles arose late and his father and Jonathan had already left the house. Giles breakfasted hurriedly and left for Lord Rowan's house to see Lavinia. He found her in the morning room.

'Giles—how nice,' she cried and came forward to greet him.

'Vinny, the most extraordinary thing— where's your grandfather?' he began in his usual hasty manner.

'Gone to meet your father and Jonathan. Why?'

'Last night as I was leaving my Club, your brother was waiting for me.'

'Roderick! Whatever for?'

'It seems—at least this is what he says—that he has never agreed with the way your parents have treated you, that he himself is very fond of you and wants to meet you to make it up with you.'

'Roderick—fond of me?' Lavinia laughed. 'Never. The only person he is fond of is himself.'

'Then you don't believe him?'

'I don't know—to be serious. After all, it is more than two years since we met. He may have changed a great deal,' she laughed again. 'I have, so it's possible he has too.'

'I suppose so,' Giles said doubtfully. 'I suggested he called on you here, but he didn't want to, because of Lord Rowan. You see, although he says he wants to be reconciled with you, he's not prepared to break with his parents.'

'So—what did he want?'

'He wants you to meet him in the Gardens this afternoon at three o'clock.'

Lavinia thought for a moment.

'Shall you go?'

'I think I will,' she said slowly. 'I should like to know exactly what it is he wants.'

'Then I shall come with you,' said Giles firmly.

'Very well,' she smiled. 'We'll solve the mystery together.'

But Giles' good intention was thwarted for when he arrived home at 'Eldon House', his mother met him in the hall.

'Your father has sent an urgent message for you to join them at the office, Giles, immediately.'

'Very well, Mama,' Giles turned on his heel and left the house at once.

His father, it seemed, wished him to meet a business contact who, they had been informed, was arriving unexpectedly by train that afternoon at one-thirty.

'Shall I be free again for two-thirty?' Giles asked worriedly, not wishing to confide in either his father or his brother, and certainly not in Lord Rowan who was present, of the reason for his question.

'I expect so,' Lord Melmoth agreed reluctantly. 'But what is so important? You know we rely on you keeping yourself available, Giles, especially just now.'

'Yes, Father, I know and I'm sorry. But it is important, or I would not ask.'

'Oh—very well then.'

Circumstances seemed to conspire to delay Giles. The train was late and when' it did arrive, Giles could not find the man he had to meet. He spent an anxious half-hour making all sorts of enquiries about the gentleman from the north who had been travelling on the train, but no one had heard of him or indeed noticed anyone who could have been such a person.

Giles returned to the Keldon Shipping Line office in a state of agitation. Not only had he failed to carry out an important meeting with a client, but also he was on the verge, if he was delayed much longer, of failing to accompany Lavinia as he had promised. To add to which, some inexplicable uneasiness made him feel that it was imperative that he should go with her to meet her brother.

Lord Melmoth, knowing nothing of the reason for Giles' apparent lack of interest in the affairs of their business, was irritated by his son's attitude. He came close to being angry with Giles until Jonathan intervened.

'Father, I am sure Giles made as many enquiries as possible, and as he appears to be anxious to be off, pray let him go. His reason is, I am sure, important.'

Giles cast an appreciative glance in Jonathan's direction.

'What is it, my boy?' his father asked in less angry tones. 'You're not in any scrape are you?'

Giles grinned momentarily. 'No,' he hesitated torn between disloyalty to his father and brother and to Lavinia. 'If you must know, I promised to take Lavinia to the Gardens. She—she wants to meet someone and I don't think it wise for her to go alone.'

He was thankful that Lord Rowan had left, for he may have asked embarrassing questions. Giles was, however, surprised at the reactions of his father and brother. The former chuckled and nodded.

'I see, playing chaperon, eh? Well, well, my boy, in that case you cannot break a promise, especially to Lavinia. Off you go.'

Jonathan said nothing but the bleak, hopeless look which crossed his face shook Giles considerably and he was still thinking about it when he turned his brougham in the direction of Lord Rowan's house.

When he arrived there, he was now more than twenty minutes late for it was almost five minutes to three. To his dismay he found that Lavinia, presumably thinking he was not coming and not wishing to miss her appointment with Roderick, had left. Fortunately Lord Rowan was not at home either, immediately, Giles made all speed to the gardens. The rendezvous had been fixed for the fountain in the centre of the park. Nearing it, Giles scanned the strolling figures—there was no sign of Lavinia, of Roderick, nor of any conveyance which either of them may have used. As the Gardens were no great distance from Lavinia's home, Giles presumed she had probably walked. He cursed himself for not having asked the servants as to how and when Miss Kelvin had left the house. As always, he had not thought of it at the time. He waited for what seemed an interminable time, but in fact only a quarter of an hour. Then he drove around the vicinity of the fountain, and, at last, in desperation he toured most of the paths of the gardens. By the time this was done it was over an hour since he had arrived there.

With one last look round the area of the fountain, he returned to Lord Rowan's house and, finding that neither Lavinia nor Lord Rowan had returned home, he went back once more to the Keldon offices. Giles was feeling sick with fear, positive that something had happened to Lavinia and that he had been instrumental in causing it to happen.

He burst into the room where he had left his father and Jonathan over an hour before, to find them almost as he had left them, discussing business and dealing with paperwork on their desks.

Giles stood for a moment in the doorway to regain his breath. He seemed to have been running and hurrying ever since lunch. Lord Melmoth and Jonathan looked up immediately on his entry. Jonathan stood up and came swiftly towards him.

'What is it, Giles? What is wrong?'

'Oh dear, what can have happened?' panted Giles, incoherent with anxiety now.

'Lavinia—is it Lavinia?' Jonathan asked urgently. 'Tell me!'

Giles nodded. 'Oh dear,' he said again, 'I should have told you before, only she seemed to want to go—why didn't she wait for me? Where can she have gone?'

'Tell me,' repeated Jonathan shaking Giles' arm.

'Giles, you're making no sense,' Lord Melmoth interrupted. 'Sit down, calm yourself and tell us exactly what has happened.'

Jonathan opened his mouth to say more, but seemed to change his mind, for he remained silent and let his hand fall from Giles' arm. Giles rubbed his arm absently where Jonathan had gripped it with such intensity.

He told them then, swiftly, beginning with his meeting with Roderick right up to the very moment he had returned to the office, a few moments before. They heard him out in silence, but he could not fail to see the anxious glances his father and brother exchanged, nor Jonathan's increasing agitation. As Giles finished his story, Jonathan, unable to restrain his anger any longer burst out,

'You fool, Giles, you absolute and utter fool! You *know* Roderick can mean Lavinia no good.'

'But . . .'

'But nothing—you should have known. Giles, if anything has happened to her, I'll—I'll horsewhip you!'

Jonathan strode from the room, whilst Giles fell miserably silent and Lord Melmoth gaped after his elder son in astonishment at the intensity of his emotional outburst.

Chapter Ten

Jonathan drove his gig at a furious pace through the streets of London, causing pedestrians to scatter in alarm, and carriage drivers to curse him whilst they struggled to calm rearing horses frightened by the commotion his speed caused. But Jonathan cared not. At last he drew up before a house in a quiet, select neighbourhood and jumped down before the vehicle had stopped entirely. He bounded up the steps three at a time, rang the bell and hammered on the door, which opened after a moment's pause. Jonathan strode in, ignoring the protestations of the butler.

'Lady Anthea—where is she?' Jonathan demanded of a servant.

'Not at home, sir, I do assure you.'

'I'll see for myself.' Angrily he opened the door of a room to the right and began methodically to search each room leading off the hall.

'Are you looking for me, Jonathan?' a voice came from the top of the stairs, and he turned to see the elegant figure of Lady Anthea, regarding him with a look of surprise, but with pleasure at this unexpected visit from her former admirer. But the look of triumph died a little when, coming down the stairs, she became aware of his expression, his eyes dark with anger, his lips pursed, his face pale and the ugly scar standing out a vivid slash down his cheek.

She was as lovely as ever, even though she was dressed completely in black in mourning for her husband. But Jonathan appeared to notice nothing about her.

'Where is she, Anthea?'

'My dear Jonathan,' she tried to pacify him, coming towards him with outstretched hands—invitingly. 'How lovely to see you.

It's been so long—too long, Jonathan,' she murmured softly, close now.

Jonathan remained totally unmoved by her wiles.

'Where is Lavinia?'

'Jonathan—I don't know what you're talking about. Why should *I* know where the girl is?'

'I think you know very well what I'm talking about—far better than I do myself.'

'I assure you I do not.' For a moment her eyes glittered dangerously, then she forced herself to laugh and put her hand on his arm.

'Come and sit down, Jonathan, and . . .'

'Tell me what you have done with her,' his voice trembled with rage and anxiety which he was trying so hard to control. He grasped her wrist suddenly and twisted her arm. She gave a little scream more out of surprise than pain.

'Jonathan! You're hurting me.'

'Where is she?' he said between his teeth.

'I don't know—I don't know.'

'You're a good liar, Anthea. I know to my cost. I believed your lies once before, remember?'

She looked into his eyes and read the coldness there, she saw at once that there could never be another chance of recapturing his affection. Angrily she shook herself free.

'I *don't* know where she is,' she said sulkily.

'But you *do* know what has happened to her, don't you?' He grasped her shoulders and shook her fiercely. 'Don't you?'

For the first time in her life she felt a pang of fear. Lady Anthea had never been so roughly treated by any man, much less one she had thought her willing slave. She realised now that his love for her—if it had been that and not merely boyish infatuation—was completely dead now. Now, from the look on his face it was apparent that he despised her.

Instead of answering his question she asked softly, regretful, almost, that she had not valued this man's affection, that she had made such a mess of her own life when it might have been so different . . .

'Do you love her, Jonathan?'

She saw the pain flicker across his face and his eyes, already angry and anxious, take on a haunted look.

'That's none of your business—just answer my questions.' But his reactions had answered her question.

She sighed. 'Her brother arranged for her to meet him in the gardens and take a drive with him.'

'And?'

'We guessed your brother would perhaps come with her so it was arranged that a message should be sent to your office about the business man arriving on the train—we know Giles does that sort of job.'

'And we fell for it,' muttered Jonathan bitterly.

'Roderick was to drive her to a certain place—I don't know where, I swear it. Her father and Lord Myron would be waiting.'

'Myron—oh my God,' Jonathan's voice was a strangled whisper.

'It's not that, Jonathan, not this time,' she said swiftly. 'Lord Myron's no longer interested in her. He—he's asked me to marry him and I have accepted.'

Despite his anxiety for Lavinia, Anthea's words caused a look of incredulity to cross his face, and even the ghost of a smile appeared at the corner of his mouth.

'Good grief, Anthea, you have a talent for marrying old men for their money.'

Her hand struck his scarred cheek, but his faint smile only broadened. 'Trying to inflict more wounds upon me, Anthea? Believe me, you no longer have the power.' Then, swiftly, his thoughts turning once more to the person uppermost in his mind. 'Have they kidnapped her?'

Lady Anthea nodded.

'Why—in Heaven's name?'

'They want to blackmail you into losing the race.'

Jonathan nodded. 'I see.'

'It isn't so much you, Jonathan, whom they are trying to blackmail as Lord Rowan. No one guessed you'd care enough about her to put her before your precious steamship.'

'What?' he paused, surprise crossing his face. 'Is that how I appear to people, totally unfeeling except for my own interests?'

'Nowadays, Jonathan, yes. Ever since this,' and her fingers touched the scar on his cheek again, but gently this time.

His shoulders sagged, the defeat in his eyes was pitiful to see, even for a cold-hearted woman of Lady Anthea's nature who only used her beauty and men's affection for her to her own advantage.

'Then what must *she* think of me,' he muttered and turning on his heel, he left the house without another word.

Lady Anthea Thorwald watched him go with a feeling unusual for her, of regret. Clearly, she saw her own life mapped out before her. She shuddered—it was not a pleasant picture.

Jonathan drove to 'Eldon House' more slowly. So many emotions crowded his mind. He did not know which way to turn to look for Lavinia. He believed, however, that Lady Anthea had told him all she knew, that she did not know where the kidnappers had taken Lavinia.

He entered the house and found Lord Melmoth and Giles had returned home. Lord Rowan, too, had arrived. They all, including Lady Melmoth, turned questionlngly towards him.

'She's been kidnapped—by her father, brother and Lord Myron.'

Lord Rowan sat down quickly, covered his face with his hands and groaned like a man who had been dealt a fatal blow. Giles' face turned white and he pressed his fist into his mouth, looking almost like a small boy about to burst into tears. Lady Melmoth gave a cry and ran to her husband who put his arm round her, but his own face bore the same expression of distress as the others.

'How did you find out, my boy?' Lord Melmoth asked Jonathan.

'I went to Lady Anthea. I thought she would be involved and though she told me that much, she says she doesn't know where they've taken her—and I think she's telling the truth.'

'She—*she* told you?' Lady Melmoth said incredulously.

'I—er—got a little—er—rough with her before she would tell me, but it worked.'

'What are we to do?' asked Giles in a tremulous voice. He looked pleadingly at his brother who returned his gaze remembering his last remark to Giles. He went over to him and put his arm about his younger brother's shoulders.

'Come, you shall help me search—we shall not rest until we've found her if we have to turn London inside out.'

Lord Rowan stood up. In a few moments he looked to have aged several years, but he had recovered his composure.

'I shall go and see—my—daughter-in-law,' Lord Rowan remarked with distaste. 'For I suppose Gervase will be unavailable.' He turned to Jonathan, for it seemed they had all looked to him to take the lead. 'Do you know exactly where they live, Eldon?'

'Yes sir. Might it be as well for us to come with you? If you do learn anything from Lady Kelvin, it may help us to know where to start.'

'Yes, yes, of course. I'd prefer it.' He sighed. 'My disreputable family is no secret from you.'

'Come, come, Rowan—take heart. Lavinia has recompensed for all that surely?' Lord Melmoth tried to comfort his friend.

'Most certainly,' Lord Rowan replied sadly. 'But now she . . .' He was unable to finish his sentence and left the room.

The Eldon family exchanged understanding looks and then the two brothers made to follow Lord Rowan.

'Hey, Jonathan,' Lord Melmoth cried as they were leaving. 'What can I do? Don't leave me here doing naught to help.'

'Come with us then, Father. The more to face her might intimidate Lady Kelvin the more.'

The streets of London through which they passed grew more and more disreputable until the carriage stopped before a tumble-down tenement building.

'So,' remarked Lord Rowan bitterly, 'they are sunk to this. What chance has the child got in hands which will kidnap their own daughter and use her as hostage?'

They went inside the building and located Lady Kelvin on the second floor. She was alone. A sluttish girl—an insult to the name 'maid' —admitted them.

The four gentlemen could not help but be shocked not only at the dreary condition of the room and shabby furniture but also in the appearance of Lady Kelvin herself. It was obvious that she was a sick woman—one look at her shrunken cheeks, her bulging eyes and the yellow colour of her skin was enough. Her claw-like fingers plucked perpetually at the shawl about her shoulders. She failed to recognise them and would not answer Lord Rowan's question as to the whereabouts of Lavinia. Her eyes looked them up and down, but it was as if she did not see them.

Jonathan turned to the girl.

'What is the matter with your mistress?'

'Queer in the 'ead, she is, sir. Been like it for a year or more now, sir. Don't speak no more, she doesn't.'

There was nothing to be gained by prolonging their stay in this place so they left immediately.

'What do we do now?' Giles said when they were once more seated in the carriage and returning to 'Eldon House'.

'I suggest we dine,' Lord Melmoth said sensibly. 'Naught's to be gained by starving ourselves, and we can discuss what to do next over dinner.'

'I couldn't eat a thing,' muttered Giles.

Jonathan and his father exchanged a glance. They had both noticed that Giles had remained silent during the whole of the journey to the Kelvins' home, and they both realised from the expression on his face that as of this moment he had grown up. This incident—in which he had played an unfortunate part through his thoughtless impetuosity—would serve to sober his wildness as the duel had Jonathan's several years perilously.

They found Lady Melmoth in a state of extreme agitation. She ran down the steps to meet them almost before their carriage had stopped.

'Rupert—a boy brought this letter a few moments ago,' she handed the letter to her husband, who glanced at her worriedly.

'I have never known you intimidated before, my love.'

'Rupert, I am so afraid for the poor child ...' and tears were evident in Lady Evelina's fine eyes.

'There, there, my dear. Wilford—the letter is addressed to you so why it was brought here I don't know.'

Lord Rowan took the letter and sighed. 'I've no doubt they are so well informed that they know our every movement.'

He tore open a single sheet and read it swiftly.

'What does it say?' demanded Jonathan impatiently.

'It reads "*Lavinia is safe and well and will remain so but only if you prevent the steamship from arriving in port first*".'

'But—but,' stuttered Giles, 'they're at sea—more than three-quarters of the way home. How can we possibly stop it?'

'We could send a ship out to meet them,' Jonathan said, his eyes darting from Lord Melmoth to Lord Rowan and back, 'to try to waylay the steamship and tell Captain Darby to allow the clipper to win.'

They all went into the house and into the drawing-room before anyone spoke.

'You would do that—see all your hopes for the future of the steamship smashed?' Lord Rowan asked slowly.

'Yes,' Jonathan said steadily.

'But these are *surely* only idle threats. They dare not harm her, dare they?'

Jonathan met Lord Rowan's gaze. 'We cannot take that risk. Lavinia's safety is worth,' he swallowed hard, 'more than any wretched boat.'

Dinner was partaken with disinterest, the attention of the diners being on the discussion of every possible action.

'We don't know how we are to reply to this note, do we?' Lord Melmoth observed. 'How do they know we shall comply with their demands? How long will they hold her?'

'Until the race is over and the clipper has won, I suppose,' said Lord Rowan heavily.

'Oh no,' Giles cried. 'That's weeks. Surely they won't keep her shut up somewhere all that time?'

There was a silence whilst they all pictured Lavinia shut up in some dingy room, bound up, perhaps, and cruelly treated.

Lady Melmoth began to cry quietly, but despairingly.

Jonathan rose from the table with the agitation of anxiety.

'Lord Rowan, can you think of anywhere—anywhere at all—where your son might think to take her?'

'No—I can't. I've tried. And with Myron involved it may be a place of his choice.'

Lady Melmoth shuddered. 'Poor Lavinia—in that man's clutches again. Oh Rupert, you don't think he'll, that Myron—will—I mean, last time . . .'

'There, there, my love. Lavinia is not the frightened creature she was then, remember she's far more able to—to defend herself.'

'It' s a possibility we cannot completely disregard,' Jonathan said, a catch in his voice, 'but perhaps it is not such a fear as you suppose.'

'Why, Jonathan?' Lady Melmoth asked.

'Lady Anthea informed me,' Jonathan continued dryly, 'that she is to *marry* Lord Myron.'

Despite their great anxiety the company allowed themselves wry smiles, unable to understand the woman's mind. Jonathan added softly, 'I think they are well-matched.'

Those few words swept away any remaining doubt there may have been in the minds of his parents and brother as to Jonathan's present feeling for Lady Anthea.

'Are we agreed then,' continued Jonathan, 'to send a ship to meet the *Lavinia* and prevent her winning?'

'I'm agreeable—most certainly,' Lord Melmoth said. 'Wilford?'

Lord Rowan sighed heavily. 'Lavinia will not wish to be the cause of you losing this race—she thinks a great deal of the steamship and I know is very proud to have it named after her.'

'It's not *her* fault, is it?' broke in Giles. 'It's mine. I'm to blame for it all.'

'Nonsense, my boy,' said Lord Rowan kindly. 'No one could be expected to contemplate such treatment from her own family. The family relationship you enjoy naturally leads you to believe that other families are similarly united.'

'But I should have thought—I should have realised after last time . . .'

'Come on, Giles,' Jonathan interrupted. 'Make yourself

useful—we'll start looking for her. But first we must send a message to the office—we are agreed, are we not, to send a message to the ship?'

Lord Rowan and Lord Melmoth exchanged a despairing glance. 'Of course,' Lord Melmoth said and Lord Rowan merely nodded, feeling, no doubt, the burden of the impending disaster which this could cause to their Company.

'I'll attend to that, Jonathan,' said Lord Melmoth.

'Very well. Father.'

He turned in the doorway. 'Lord Rowan, I presume you wish all this to be kept secret.'

The Earl sighed deeply. 'I begin to think I should no longer protect my son, but the reflection on Lavinia ...'

Jonathan nodded. 'If we could find her ourselves it would save her, and you, a great deal of embarrassment. Come, Giles.'

The two brothers left to begin their search and whilst they both feared that this was of little use, neither of them could sit idly by and wait for something to happen. During the hours of darkness whilst they rode through the deserted streets, the two brothers felt themselves drawn inexplicably closer together, even though they were already, by most standards, singularly united as brothers. Jonathan's earlier outburst of blame against Giles was forgotten, each acknowledging that it was said in a moment of emotional distress. Giles, though readily accepting that he was to blame, and therefore that Jonathan's threat was fully justified, wondered vaguely whether Jonathan did—whether he realised it himself or not—love Lavinia in the same way in which she loved him. Giles began to hope that he did. The night passed without any accomplishment, and the brothers returned home to breakfast weary-eyed but not desirous of sleep.

Rowan and Melmoth, too, it seemed, had not slept, nor had they left Lord Melmoth's study all night. They had discussed the matter through the night. Only Lady Melmoth had been persuaded to retire to bed, though it was obvious that she too had found sleep impossible.

Conversation was little at breakfast for no one wished to indulge in idle chatter and all discussion on the one topic which held them totally absorbed had been exhausted. As the meal was ending, the butler hurried in with a note.

'This has just been pushed through the door, sir.'

'Did you see who brought it?' Lord Melmoth asked sharply, whilst Jonathan and Giles sprang up and hurried to the window.

'No, sir, I am afraid I did not. I have only just seen it on the floor just inside the main door, sir.'

'There's' no sign of anyone leaving,' Jonathan remarked.

'It says,' read Lord Rowan, ' "*the girl is safe—at the moment—but you are delaying taking the necessary action. Perhaps you do not value her life?*" '

An explosion of oaths from the gentlemen greeted the last words, whilst Lady Evelina gave a cry of alarm.

'Wilford,' she gasped, 'surely they would not—dare not . . .'

Lord Rowan sat with his shoulders hunched. He looked at her sadly. 'I no longer know what to think, Evelina,' he said heavily.

'Oh, 'tis only a threat, my dear,' Lord Melmoth tried to comfort her, but his words failed to convince anyone in the room.

'They should know by now that we're planning to send a ship out to meet the *Lavinia*,' cried Giles. 'Why do they say we have taken no action?'

'I would imagine this was written last night—late into the night probably—and has only just reached us by messenger,' Jonathan said.

'Then they could be some distance away?' Giles suggested.

'Presuming the note was written from where they are holding Vinny, yes.'

Giles ran his hand through his hair distractedly.

'If only, if only . . .'

'When will the ship leave?' put in Lady Melmoth.

'Unfortunately, not before tomorrow,' Jonathan replied. 'We had nothing ready to sail and it cannot possibly leave before noon tomorrow.'

'Do you think they will release her once they know you've sent a ship out?' she asked.

'No, I don't,' Jonathan said, 'for that will not be proof enough for them that we mean to lose the race.'

Later that morning the news that the steamship was now well ahead of the clipper only caused the family greater alarm, when normally they would have been filled with exhilaration.

Jonathan and Giles searched the streets again all that day and when they returned home for dinner late in the evening their dispiritedness and tiredness were self-evident. Worry robbed them all of their appetites, so that the dishes left the table sometimes almost untouched.

'The number of derelict buildings we've seen,' groaned Giles. 'Do you really think that's the sort of place they'll keep her in?'

'They'll not keep her in the obvious places—what else can we do but just look and hope,' murmured Jonathan.

As the family and Lord Rowan moved through the hall from the dining-room, Jonathan went towards the front door.

'My dear, you're not going out again?' Lady Melmoth said.

'I cannot stay here whilst there's a chance, however remote, that we might find her.'

Giles followed him.

'No, Giles, you stay here, you're tired and . . .'

'I'm coming with you, Jonathan,' and the tone in his voice refuted all argument.

Out into the darkness they went side by side once more.

'What do you think of trying one or two of the roads leading right out of London?' Giles said. 'So far we've just toured the city streets.'

'Yes, I think perhaps you're right.' He sighed. 'I don't really think there's much hope we shall find her but I can't sit and wait.'

'Nor me.'

They took the road which led ultimately to Dover and, after some time, came to the suburbs.

'This is a part we haven't been before,' said Jonathan and they sat one either side of the vehicle watching out.

They drove for two hours.

'How far do you think we should go?' muttered Giles, rubbing his shoulder which ached from sitting in the same position so long.

'I don't know what to . . . Wilkes, stop!' Jonathan roared suddenly.

'What is it . . .?' Giles started to say, but Jonathan had flung open the door of the brougham and leapt out. Giles followed him and saw his brother running along the road towards the small figure of a girl, her white dress shining in the moonlight.

He heard Jonathan's cry of relief.

'Vinny, Vinny.'

'Oh Jonathan, Jonathan,' Giles heard her faint cry and saw her stretch out her arms towards Jonathan before she began to fall.

Jonathan reached her and caught her in his arms.

'My lovely Vinny, what have they done to you, my darling?' he said huskily.

He picked her up and carried her to the brougham. Her arms were about his neck, her head on his shoulder and a gentle smile on her lips. Hardly comprehending his endearments, she knew, nevertheless, that she was safe in his arms.

'Jonathan, I knew you would come.'

Without warning she fainted.

Jonathan placed her carefully in the brougham and they turned with all speed for home.

'Will she come round?' Giles asked anxiously, as Jonathan hovered over her.

'Yes, in a minute I expect. It will be more fatigue than anything I suppose.'

'How did she come to be here on the road, do you think?'

'We shall only know when she can tell us. Vinny, Vinny, come along.'

Her eyelids flickered.

'Where . . .' she sat up sharply. 'Don't you lay one finger . . .' she began.

'Vinny, steady, it's me,' Jonathan said.

'Oh Jonathan!' She flung her arms about his neck. 'I remember now, just for a moment I thought I was back there.'

Jonathan sat beside her, his arms about her. She leaned against him and sighed contentedly.

'Do you feel all right now?'

'A bit shaky. You don't mind if I—go to sleep. I'm so very, very tired.'

Before they could reply, she was asleep.

'Has she fainted again?' Giles asked.

'No she's sleeping now.'

The return journey was accomplished in an hour for their outward journey had been purposely slow.

Lord Rowan and Lord Melmoth were still up when Jonathan carried the sleeping girl into the house.

'Jonathan—thank God you've found her,' Lord Rowan hurried forward. He put his hand on Jonathan's shoulder in a gesture of gratitude too deep for words.

'Is she—hurt?'

'No, no, I don't think so,' Jonathan replied softly, his eyes never leaving Vinny's face as he laid her gently on the sofa. But now that they could all see her better, they saw that her face was marked with small scratches and an ugly bruise on her forehead. Jonathan felt his anger rise against her captors, that they should have caused her to be hurt in any way at all.

'Fetch your mother, Giles, she's gone to bed,' Lord Melmoth instructed.

As Giles hurried away the other three men stood looking down at the sleeping girl with thankfulness in their hearts. Jonathan felt Lord Rowan's hand upon his shoulder again and turned to see tears in the older man's eyes.

'My boy, I can never thank you enough,' and his voice broke.

'I shall have all the thanks I need as long as she is unharmed,' he murmured, and Lord Rowan looked into his eyes for a moment and saw for himself the depth of Jonathan's feelings for his grand-daughter. He nodded understandingly.

Lady Melmoth entered with Giles following her.

'Oh, poor child,' she said at once. 'Look at the state of her clothes. Jonathan, carry her upstairs and put her in my bed. Giles, send for Doctor Benning. Rupert, show Lord Rowan to the guest room. You must rest now, Wilford.'

Lady Melmoth was once again her usual self, her one thought being to care for the girl once again in her charge almost in the same way as before.

Jonathan carried Lavinia upstairs and having laid her gently on the bed, he found himself shooed out by his mother whilst she and her maid tried to rouse the sleeping girl and help her undress.

The door closed behind him shutting him out. He smiled ruefully to himself—naturally his mother was right, but he had a compelling need to stay with Lavinia, never to let her out of his sight again.

Later, when the doctor had announced that her only injuries were scratches and a few bruises, and, of course exhaustion. Lady Melmoth reported that Lavinia was ready to sleep again after the doctor had examined her, but that she was, although desperately tired, insisting that she should be allowed to see Giles before she slept.

'Now, only a moment, Giles,' Lady Melmoth told him. 'The foolish girl will not rest until she has seen you.'

'Me?' Giles asked incredulously. 'Are you sure she said me and not . . .' He hesitated and glanced quickly at Jonathan.

Lady Melmoth, not understanding that Giles, knowing as he did of Lavinia's love for Jonathan, could not believe that it was he and not Jonathan for whom she was asking, replied, 'Naturally, she wants to see her grandfather, and everyone, later when she's rested. She's so weary, poor child, but she is adamant she must see you.'

Giles saw the hurt in Jonathan's eyes, saw the gentle smile fade from his brother's lips and, in a moment, saw that Jonathan was convinced Lavinia's first thought was for Giles and not for him. Giles sighed. Now it would be even more difficult to bring them together, he thought.

Giles found Lavinia drowsy, willing herself to keep awake until she had seen him.

'Giles—I just wanted to tell you—not to blame yourself. It was my fault—but I know you'll have been—feeling responsible. Don't worry any more.'

Her eyelids closed.

Lavinia slept soundly through the night and did not wake until four o'clock the following afternoon, when, except for the scratches and bruises on her face and hands, she seemed fully recovered and insisted on rising and dressing for dinner.

When she came downstairs, she found her way firstly to Jonathan's study, hoping to catch him alone. The memory of his words when he had found her had remained with her and she could not help but hope that they may mean something. She opened the door and found him sitting at his desk his head in his hands. Slowly he looked up.

'Why, Lavinia.' He rose from his desk, but she could not fail to notice his formal use of her name and the reserve in his manner. 'I am pleased to see you have made a swift recovery.' Lavinia sat down in the chair near the fireplace and he sat down at his desk once more. She looked at him for a long time without speaking. He returned her gaze for a moment then he looked away.

'Those—scratches and bruises—how did they happen?' A note of sharpness had crept into his tone and she noticed his hand, lying on the desk, clenched and unclenched nervously.

'I'm not sure—I kept walking into hedges, I think. I escaped and walked all last night—that's why I was so tired. No, the night before that, I escaped—oh dear I've lost track of time.'

He looked at her in astonishment as she continued.

'I've no idea where they took me—but it was into the country. I was completely lost when I did escape and so afraid they'd come after me that every time I heard something I ducked into a field or into a ditch—hence all the scratches.'

'Did you walk all the way back?'

'No—I escaped the night before last and walked until daylight. I think it would be about mid-day when a carriage stopped and the one passenger was kind enough to bring me so far—then I walked again until you found me.'

'Did they—your captors, I mean—did they mistreat you?'

She glanced down at her hands in her lap and whilst she did so, Jonathan risked another glance at her. It was all he could do to control his emotions, to stop himself taking her in his arms. Last night he had admitted to himself that he loved her. In the darkness he had relived in thought all the time he had known her. It seemed, now that he had admitted it to himself at last, that he had loved her for a long time. He did not believe that it had been 'love at first sight', but there was no doubt that on that very first evening—so long ago it seemed now—in her parents' house, he had even then felt the beginning of affection. Why else should he have worried about her visit to Myron? Why else should he have been so thankful that her grandfather had taken care of her? He remembered her year in France when he had looked forward to her letters without knowing why himself, without realising why the knowledge that she had met and continued to meet Francis Selwyn distressed him. He recalled the ball when Lady Anthea had so skilfully spoilt the entire evening for him by sending Lord Selwyn to dance with Lavinia. Then, he had only known that he had wanted to be with Vinny, to dance with her and look upon her smiling face and marvel at the change from the waif she had been to the beautiful young girl in his arms. He had not recognised these feelings as the beginning of love. Jonathan had never been sure what it had been that Lavinia had been trying to say to him before Lord Selwyn had whirled her away. He had thought at the time she would prefer Francis Selwyn's company, but now he was not so sure. She had spent the last winter in Warwickshire with no apparent pining for city life and yet, on their last visit the way she had looked at him when Giles had mentioned Lord Selwyn's visits to Lady Anthea had again made him wonder whether she was fond of Francis Selwyn.

Then there was always Giles. Can I be jealous of my own brother? Jonathan had asked himself. In the darkness he had smiled sadly to himself. Giles was the one person to whom he could give Lavinia—if they loved each other—and not be completely heartbroken himself. She was certainly fond of Giles and he of her, but surely if they were in love, it would be acknowledged by now. Yet it was Giles she had asked to see first tonight, he had thought. Sleeplessly he had tossed and turned all night. Giles was certainly more likely to be able to win her love, Jonathan told himself. How could he, Jonathan, some ten years older than her, with an ugly scar down his face, hope to be worthy of her notice? If she were in love with any man, it must be either Giles or Francis Selwyn, he had told himself. In the cold light of dawn he had given up all thought of declaring his love to her. Now, as she sat before him, it was almost more than he could bear to see her sitting there, her lovely face marked by cruel scratches and a bruise on her forehead.

'No, not really,' she was saying in answer to his question regarding her captors' treatment of her. 'Jonathan,' her brown eyes sought his. 'Your mother told me you were going to send a message to the steamship telling them to lose the race.'

There was a pause.

'Of course—what did you expect we should do? That was what they demanded.'

'You would have done that—for me?' she whispered, her eyes glowing.

'Of course,' he said abruptly. Fear that he would betray his feelings for her made his tone brusque. 'I would do it for anyone. People are more important than ships.'

Though he spoke the truth, his words told only the half of it.

The light of hope died in her eyes. 'Of course,' was all she said.

There was a pause before she said anxiously, 'The message didn't go, did it? We shall still win?'

Despite the heaviness in his heart, her faith in the steamship pleased and amused him.

He smiled. 'The ship we were going to send out could not leave before noon today—so we were able to prevent it sailing.'

'I'm glad—I would have felt awful if—if you'd—we'd lost the race because of me.'

'I've told you,' he said, 'that wouldn't have mattered a jot as long as it would have ensured your safety.' His tone was a little sharp again. He could not bear to look at her sitting there looking so forlorn over the thought that he put the steamship before her welfare. If she only knew the truth, he thought, that he would see their whole fleet at the bottom of the sea before he would see a hair of her head harmed. He got up restlessly, afraid to meet her gaze, afraid she would see the passion in his eyes and be embarrassed by it.

She stood up. 'I must go—it's almost time for dinner.'

He went and opened the door for her, a tight, wary smile at the corner of his mouth. She passed out of the room close to him but her eyes were downcast and she did not look up at him.

Over dinner, the family demanded to hear the full story of the kidnapping.

'It was wrong of me to have gone without Giles—I realise that now. I do hope you don't blame him in any way,' she turned her clear gaze towards Lord Melmoth. 'I've already told him he is not to blame himself. Well—I went to the Gardens and Roderick was waiting for me near the fountain. We talked for a few moments—oh, he spun me a fine tale,' she laughed. 'I was completely taken in.'

Merriment was in her tone, but her listeners could not share her mirth.

'After a while he suggested we take a short drive. As, by that time, I was fairly sure his attempts at reconciliation were genuine, I consented.'

'We left the park and drove for only a short distance. We slowed a little and two men jumped into the carriage and sat either side of me. Before I could utter a word or realise what was happening, they had tied a kerchief about my mouth and secured my hands behind my back.'

She paused and turned back the cuff of her sleeve to reveal the tender skin on her wrists still bore the bruises and soreness of those bonds.

'None too gently,' she smiled ruefully, 'whilst Roderick just laughed. Then the driver whipped up the horses and we journeyed for what seemed an intolerable distance. I have no idea where we were for they drew the blinds down over the windows so I could not see out. At last we stopped and I was blind-folded too and led into a building—up numerous stairs and pushed into an attic and left alone.'

'Didn't they bring you any food?' Giles asked.

'Nothing. I must have been there for several hours before I managed to free the bonds round my wrist on a rusty nail. I had lost all account of time. Fortunately for me they had not bothered to secure the door. It was frightening trying to get out of that place—I was so afraid one of them would come at any moment. Anyway, I crept down the stairs in complete darkness and somehow—though I really couldn't tell you how—I found a door into the open air.

'Then I just ran as far as I could—I did look back once—the place seemed to be a derelict farm as far as I could see.' She shrugged and spread her hands. 'Then I just kept walking until the carriage stopped and brought me part of the way, then I walked again until Jonathan and Giles found me.'

Though Lavinia, in the telling of her story, had minimised the danger and the treatment of her captors, no one was in any doubt as to the frightening circumstances in which the girl had found herself.

'The sooner we return to 'Avonridge', my dear, the better,' Lord Rowan said.

'But Grandfather,' Lavinia cried, her eyes wide, 'we must stay until the steamship has won. I must!'

'Do you still mean you're interested in the race after all that's happened to you because of it?' Lord Melmoth enquired in surprise.

'Of course I am—it's nothing to do with the steamship, is it?'

Only Giles of their number realised that it was not just the ship itself but because it was Jonathan's pride and joy which caused Lavinia's unfailing interest.

So Lord Rowan and Lavinia remained in London until the *Lavinia* returned. The excitement grew in the city as day by day the ships drew nearer. Wagers were taken as to which ship would win. Rumours said that the *Lavinia* was first, then another said that the clipper was far ahead. The ships were to dock at the East India Docks, and the last day, when it was still undecided as to which would win, found the Eldon family, Lord Rowan and Lavinia near the docks awaiting the end of the race. They were able to find a spot where they could see some distance down the river and were joined by several other spectators, for the race had caused great interest in the city.

Anxiety was again the over-riding emotion. With Lavinia safe again, and the message never sent to the steamship, there had been no setback in the race itself. Now all their thoughts were on it. Would their ship win and show the way to the future, or would the clipper come sailing in defiantly, smashing all Jonathan's hopes and dreams and bring, if not total ruin to the Company, at least a financial disaster?

Jonathan remained motionless, his only sign of anxiety seeming to be his total engrossment in watching for the steamship. Giles paced up and down muttering to himself, alternating between confident elation and despondency. Lavinia, her mood matching Jonathan's, one of quiet but tense expectancy, went to stand beside him.

He was painfully aware of her presence, though he gave every appearance of being wholly absorbed in watching for his steamship. She, for her part, was willing her namesake to win for Jonathan's sake. Suddenly she clutched his arm in excitement. Her sharp eyes had seen a shape looming up in the distance moving steadily towards them. Silently, she pointed, her hand returning to clasp Jonathan's as they stood breathlessly watching the ship move nearer, waiting until they could be sure . . .

Jonathan's whisper was for Lavinia alone. 'It's your ship, Vinny, it is the *Lavinia*.'

'Oh Jonathan, it is—I know it is,' she turned to him, tears running down her face. He looked down at her smiling tenderly.

Then a shout went up amongst the crowd.

'It's the steamship—It's the *Lavinia*.'

People cheered, whilst Lavinia laughed and cried with happiness and Jonathan continued to gaze down at her.

'It's our ship, it's our ship!' The boisterous Giles bounced up and whirled Lavinia round to embrace her, lifting her completely off the ground. When she laughingly admonished him and demanded to be put down, she turned to find that Jonathan had disappeared into the crowd.

It was indeed the steamship which had won the race and all the anxiety of the past months and weeks was over and ahead lay the fulfilment of all Jonathan's plans.

A little sadly, after all the excitement, Lavinia turned away. She knew she had no part in those plans and even though she knew the Eldons were her dearest friends, the future held no bright prospect for her without Jonathan.

Lord Rowan insisted that they should return to 'Avonridge' the next day.

'You're looking so pale my clear child,' he said. 'After your frightening experience and the excitement of the race, it's too much for you. Back to 'Avonridge' we go where you will take a good long rest.'

Lavinia was not completely sorry to return to the place she regarded as her home for although she was leaving Jonathan, she realised he would now be so busy again that she would see little of him even if they did remain in town.

As they travelled through the countryside a few days later towards Warwickshire, her grandfather said conversationally, 'It's time you were thinking about marriage, my dear.'

'Oh no. Grandfather,' Lavinia's swift reply was scandalised.

'Not that I want to lose you, my love,' his kind eyes twinkled, 'but it is my dearest wish to see you happily settled.' His tone sobered. 'Life has little meaning unless you have a loved one to share it.'

Lavinia knew he was thinking of the idyllic years he had known with her grandmother. But how could she tell him she already knew this—how could she explain to him that there was only one person with whom she wished to spend her life? So she remained silent, hoping that this was merely idle chatter on his part, and not the beginning of a campaign to see her well-married.

Four weeks passed in which she fully recovered and all the marks of her unfortunate experience disappeared without trace. She thought her grandfather had forgotten his words about marriage, so she was surprised when he announced one morning at breakfast.

'I am expecting some guests to arrive this afternoon, my dear, one of whom will be a young man who, I believe, wishes to pay court to you.'

'But Grandfather, I don't want . . .'

'Lavinia, you will oblige me by receiving this young man. I shall be most seriously displeased if you are uncivil to him.'

She looked at her grandfather. She had never heard him speak so sternly and his face gave no sign that he was anything but serious,

'Yes, Grandfather,' she said meekly, and left the table without looking back so she missed seeing the mischievous twinkle Lord Rowan allowed himself behind her back.

She spent the morning discarding all manner of wild ideas for escape from the preposterous idea that she should allow a complete stranger to court her. By mid-afternoon, however, she was resigned to the fact that she must, at least, receive the young gentleman for she could not so easily displease her grandfather after all his goodness to her.

Mid-afternoon, which was the expected time of arrival for the guests, found Lavinia in her favourite spot, her grandmother's small garden. Seated on the white painted garden seat, watching the sparkling fountain, she could not feel the peace and happiness she usually found in this secluded spot. She sighed. She supposed she must return to the house and meet her grandfather's guests and her would-be suitor.

'Vinny.' The soft tones of a well-known voice startled her reveries. She jumped to her feet and turned to see him standing at the entrance to the enclosed garden.

'Jonathan!'

'May I join you?'

'Oh—yes—of course, but . . .' she hesitated as he came towards her. Her eyes searched his face.

'I didn't know you were coming. Grandfather is expecting guests but . . .' Again she paused, hardly daring to believe the impossible idea forming in her mind.

His smile, so beloved by her, his sideways smile was at the corner of his mouth. 'Yes,' he said, 'Lord Rowan is expecting guests—the Eldon family.'

'Then who—who is the young man he said—he said . . .'

Jonathan's smile faded a little and a wary look came into his eyes. He seemed ill-at-ease.

'Vinny—I am the young man who wishes to . . . to . . .'

The look upon her face would have answered his question even before he asked it for radiance flooded her eyes, but he had looked down as if almost afraid to meet her gaze. She stepped closer to him, her eyes never leaving his face.

'Vinny, Vinny, my love,' he took her hands in his and raised them to his lips. 'I love you so much—I know you can never love me—but do you think . . .?'

'Jonathan,' she said softly, 'why do you think I could never love you?'

Now he looked into her eyes again searching their depths, puzzled.

'Giles said . . .' he hesitated.

'Giles! Oh and he promised,' she cried, but not angry now. For now she had heard those magical, unbelievable words from Jonathan—words she had never dared to hope she might hear—she could forgive anyone anything.

'He didn't tell me who it is.'

'Who is what?' she asked. 'Now, tell me *exactly* what Giles did say.'

'Well, I wouldn't be here saying this but for him,' Jonathan admitted. 'We were talking about you and he said "poor Vinny, she'll never make a happy marriage." I asked him what he meant and he said, "she's given her heart to some worthless fellow who never even notices she exists and doesn't deserve her." Vinny, I know I am a poor substitute but I do love you so and I'll try to make you happy if . . .'

Lavinia laid her finger against his lips and laughed softly.

'Jonathan, shall I tell you who that "worthless fellow" is?'

A look of pain crossed his eyes. 'If you must, but I think I'd really rather not know.'

She moved even closer and laid her cheek against his shoulder.

'He is you.'

There was a pause, so long that she began to think he had not heard so she went on. 'Giles knew I loved you a long time ago, even before I went to France. Strangely enough, it was just here, in this garden, he found out. He came to look for me and I was sitting here sketching,' she drew back and looked up at him. 'Sketching dozens of portraits of you—and he guessed just why my pencil kept drawing your face.'

'You really *mean* it? I thought—when Giles said that, that perhaps it was Lord Selwyn or,' he smiled ruefully, 'even Giles himself.'

She could still read the disbelief in his voice and on his face.

'I'll spend the rest of my life convincing you that it *is* you,' she said.

'But I'm so much older than you and—and there's this.' His fingers touched the scar on his face.

'Oh that,' she said casually. 'That's a sign of maturity. We've all got scars, Jonathan, left by the pains of growing up, but they're not all visible like yours, but they're there for all that. And fancy you thinking I could have fallen for the man who caused you so much unhappiness.'

Jonathan smiled—really smiled—and gathered her into his arms.

'Well, well, well,' said a voice behind them and they turned to see Giles grinning at them round the corner of the hedge which enclosed the garden. 'I thought I'd *never* get you two together. I had the devil's own job, Vinny, getting it across to him without actually breaking my word to you.'

He came and stood before them grinning happily.

'You always seem to come at the wrong moment, my boy,' Jonathan drawled, but Lavinia heard the amusement in his tone. 'You've done it before—frequently.'

'Oh I know, but that was to save Vinny embarrassment usually.'

Giles stood with his back to the fountain quite close to the edge. The same thought must have flashed through the minds of Lavinia and Jonathan simultaneously for they looked at each other, smiled mischievously and moved towards Giles, hand in hand.

'A "worthless fellow" is he, Giles?' Lavinia laughed.

'What shall we do with him, Vinny?' Jonathan asked.

'I don't know.'

They moved forward again.

Giles took a step backwards and another.

'Now, wait a minute, aaah ...'

With flailing arms he fell backwards and sat down in the pool whilst the fountain showered over him.

'You—you—wait,' he spluttered.

Jonathan and Lavinia burst out laughing, turned and, hand in hand, ran from the garden and across the smooth lawns to the house, whilst Giles sat beneath the fountain and smiled benignly after them.

Lightning Source UK Ltd.
Milton Keynes UK
UKOW04f0216221214

243522UK00003B/46/P